R0110918828

02/2019

Also by Linda Howard

A Lady of the West
Angel Creek
The Touch of Fire
Heart of Fire
Dream Man
After the Night
Shades of Twilight
Son of the Morning
Kill and Tell
Now You See Her
All the Queen's Men
Mr. Perfect
Open Season

Published by POCKET BOOKS

LINDA HOWARD

STRANGERS *in the* NIGHT

Lake of Dreams

Blue Moon

White Out

POCKET BOOKS

New York   London   Toronto   Sydney

This book is a work of fiction. Names, characters, places and
incidents are products of the author's imagination or are used
fictitiously. Any resemblance to actual events or locales or persons,
living or dead, is entirely coincidental.

POCKET BOOKS, a division of Simon & Schuster, Inc.
1230 Avenue of the Americas, New York, NY 10020

Lake of Dreams copyright © 1995 by Linda Howington
White Out copyright © 1997 by Linda Howington
Blue Moon copyright © 1999 by Linda Howington

Originally published in hardcover in 2001 by Pocket Books

ISBN 978-1-4516-2813-5

First Pocket Books paperback printing November 2002

10 9 8 7 6 5

POCKET and colophon are registered trademarks of
Simon & Schuster, Inc.

For information regarding special discounts for bulk purchases,
please contact Simon & Schuster Special Sales at 1-800-456-6798
or business@simonandschuster.com

Cover design by Lisa Litwack; front cover photo © Kazutomo Kawai/Photonica

Printed in the U.S.A.

These titles were previously published individually by Pocket Books

Contents

LAKE OF DREAMS

1

His eyes were like jewels, *aquamarines as deep and vivid as the sea, burning through the mist that enveloped him.* They glittered down at her, the expression in them so intense that she was frightened, and struggled briefly in his grasp. He soothed her, his voice rough with passion as he controlled her struggles, stroking and caressing until she was once more quivering with delight, straining upward to meet him. His hips hammered rhythmically at her, driving deep. His powerful body was bare, his iron muscles moving like oiled silk under his sweaty skin. The mist from the lake swirled so thickly around them that she couldn't see him clearly, could only feel him, inside and without, possessing her so fiercely and completely that she knew she would never

3

be free of him. His features were lost in the mist, no matter how she strained her eyes to see him, no matter how she cried out in frustration. Only the hot jewels of his eyes burned through, eyes that she had seen before, through other mists—

Thea jerked awake, her body quivering with the echo of passion . . . and completion. Her skin was dewed with sweat, and she could hear her own breathing, coming hard and fast at first, then gradually slowing as her heartbeat settled into its normal pace. The dream always drained her of strength, left her wrung out and boneless from exhaustion.

She felt shattered, unable to think, overcome by both panic and passion. Her loins throbbed as if she had just made love; she twisted on the tangled sheets, pressing her thighs together to try to negate the sensation of still having him within her. *Him.* Nameless, faceless, but always *him.*

She stared at the dim early-morning light that pressed against the window, a graying so fragile that it scarcely penetrated the glass. There was no need to look at the clock; the dream always came in the dark, silent hour before dawn, and ended at the first approach of light.

It's just a dream, she told herself, reaching for any possible comfort. *Only a dream.*

But it was unlike any dream she'd ever had before.

She thought of it as a single dream, and yet the individual episodes were different. They—it—had begun almost a month before. At first she had simply thought of it as a weird dream, singularly vivid and frightening, but still only a dream. Then it had come again the next night. And the next. And every night since, until she dreaded going to sleep. She had tried setting her alarm to go off early, to head the dream off at the pass, so to speak, but it hadn't worked. Oh, the alarm had gone off, all right; but as she'd been lying in bed grumpily mourning the lost sleep and steeling herself to actually get up, the dream had come anyway. She had felt awareness fade, had felt herself slipping beneath the surface of consciousness into that dark world where the vivid images held sway. She'd tried to fight, to stay awake, but it simply hadn't been possible. Her heavy eyes had drifted shut, and he was there again . . .

He was angry with her, furious that she'd tried to evade him. His long dark hair swirled around his shoul-

ders, the strands almost alive with the force of his tem-
per. His eyes . . . oh, God, his eyes, as vivid as the
dream, a hot blue-green searing through the clouds of
mosquito netting that draped her bed. She lay very still,
acutely aware of the cool linen sheets beneath her, of the
heavy scents of the tropical night, of the heat that made
even her thin nightgown feel oppressive . . . and most of
all of her flesh quivering in frightened awareness of the
man standing in the night-shadowed bedroom, staring at
her through the swath of netting.

Frightened, yes, but she also felt triumphant. She
had known it would come to this. She had pushed him,
dared him, taunted him to this very outcome, this devil's
bargain she would make with him. He was her enemy.
And tonight he would become her lover.

He came toward her, his warrior's training evident in
the grace and power of his every move. "You tried to evade
me," he said, his voice as dark as the evening thunder. His
fury rippled around him, almost visible in its potency.
"You played your games, deliberately arousing me to the
mindlessness of a stallion covering a mare . . . and now
you dare try to hide from me? I should strangle you."

She rose up on one elbow. Her heart was pounding in
her chest, painfully thudding against her ribs, and she
felt as if she might faint. But her flesh was awakening to

his nearness, discounting the danger. "I was afraid," she said simply, disarming him with the truth.

He paused, and his eyes burned more vividly than before. "Damn you," he whispered. "Damn both of us." Then his powerful warrior's hands were on the netting, freeing it, draping it over her upper body. The insubstantial wisp settled over her like a dream itself, and yet it still blurred his features, preventing her from seeing him clearly. His touch, when it came, wrenched a soft, surprised sound from her lips. His hands were rough and hot, sliding up her bare legs in a slow caress, lifting her nightgown out of the way. Violent hunger, all the more fierce for being unwilling, emanated from him as he stared at the shadowed juncture of her thighs.

So it was to be that way, then, she thought, and braced herself. He intended to take her virginity without preparing her. So be it. If he thought he could make her cry out in pain and shock, he would be disappointed. He was a warrior, but she would show him that she was his equal in courage.

He took her that way, pulled to the edge of the bed and with only her lower body bared, and the mosquito netting between them. He took her with anger, and with tenderness. He took her with a passion that seared her, with a completeness that marked her forever as his. And, in the end, she did cry out. That triumph was his, after all. But her cries weren't of pain, but of pleasure and fulfillment, and a glory she hadn't known existed.

That was the first time he'd made love to her, the first time she'd awakened still trembling from a climax so sweet and intense that she'd wept in the aftermath, huddled alone in her tangled bed and longing for more. The first time, but definitely not the last.

Thea got out of bed and walked to the window, restlessly rubbing her hands up and down her arms as she stared out at the quiet courtyard of her apartment building and waited for dawn to truly arrive, for the cheerful light to banish the lingering, eerie sense of unreality. Was she losing her mind? Was this how insanity began, this gradual erosion of reality until one was unable to tell what was real and what wasn't? Because the here and now was what didn't feel real to her anymore, not as real as the dreams that ushered in the dawn. Her work was suffering; her concentration was shot. If she worked for anyone but herself, she thought wryly, she would be in big trouble.

Nothing in her life had prepared her for this. Everything had been so *normal,* so Cleaverish.

Great parents, a secure home life, two brothers who had, despite all earlier indications, grown up to be nice, interesting men whom she adored. Nothing traumatic had happened to her when she was growing up; there had been the tedium of school, the almost suffocating friendships youngsters seem to need the usual wrangles and arguments, and the long, halcyon summer days spent at the lake. Every summer, her courageous mother would pack the station wagon and bravely set forth to the summer house, where she would ride herd on three energetic kids for most of the summer. Her father would drive up every weekend, and would take some of his vacation there, too. Thea remembered long, hot days of swimming and fishing, of bees buzzing in the grass, birdsong, fireflies winking in the dusk, crickets and frogs chirping, the plop of a turtle into the water, the mouthwatering smell of hamburgers cooking over charcoal. She remembered being bored, and fretting to go back home, but by the time summer would come again she'd be in a fever to get back to the lake

If anything in her life was unusual, it was her chosen occupation, but she enjoyed painting houses. She was willing to tackle any paint job, inside or out, and customers seemed to love her attention to detail. She was also getting more and more mural work, as customers learned of that particular talent and asked her to transform walls. Even her murals were cheerfully normal; nothing mystic or tortured there. So why had she suddenly begun having these weird time-period dreams, featuring the same faceless man, night after night after night?

In the dreams, his name varied. He was Marcus, and dressed as a Roman centurion. He was Luc, a Norman invader. He was Neill, he was Duncan . . . he was so many different men she should never have been able to remember the names, and yet she did. He called her different names in the dreams, too: Judith, Willa, Moira, Anice. She was all of those women, and all of those women were the same. And he was always the same, no matter his name.

He came to her in the dreams, and when he made love to her, he took more than her body. He invaded her soul, and filled her with a longing that never quite left, the sense that she was somehow incomplete without him. The pleasure was so shattering, the sensations so real, that when she had awakened the first time and lain there weeping, she had fearfully reached down to touch herself, expecting to feel the wetness of his seed. It hadn't been there, of course. He didn't exist, except in her mind.

Her thirtieth birthday was less than a week away, and in all those years she had never felt as intensely about a real man as she did about the chimera who haunted her dreams.

She couldn't keep her mind on her work. The mural she'd just finished for the Kalmans had lacked her customary attention to detail, though Mrs. Kalman had been happy with it. Thea knew it hadn't been up to her usual standards, even if Mrs. Kalman didn't. She had to stop dreaming about him. Maybe she should see a therapist, or perhaps even a psychiatrist. But everything in her rebelled against that idea, against recounting those dreams to a stranger. It would be like making love in public.

But she had to do something. The dreams were becoming more intense, more frightening. She had developed such a fear of water that, yesterday, she had almost panicked when driving over a bridge.

She, who had always loved water sports of any kind, and who swam like a fish! But now she had to steel herself to even look at a river or lake, and the fear was growing worse.

In the last three dreams, they had been at the lake. *Her* lake, where she had spent the wonderful summers of her childhood. He had invaded her home turf, and she was suddenly more frightened than she could ever remember being before. It was as if he had been stalking her in her dreams, inexorably moving closer and closer to a conclusion that she already knew.

Because, in her dreams, only sometimes did he make love to her. Sometimes he killed her.

2

The summer house was the same, but oddly diminished by time. Seen through a child's eyes, it had been a spacious, slightly magical place, a house where fun and laughter were commonplace, a house made for the long, glorious summers. Thea sat in her car and stared at it, feeling love and a sense of peace well up to overcome her fear at actually being here, at the scene of her most recent dreams. Nothing but good times were associated with this place. At the age of fourteen, she had received her first kiss, standing with Sammy Somebody there in the shadow of the weeping willow. She'd had a wild crush on Sammy for that entire summer, and now she couldn't even remember his last name! So much for true love.

Now she saw that the house was small, and in need of a paint job. She smiled, thinking that she could take care of that little chore while she was here. The grass was knee-high, and the swing, hanging from a thick branch of the huge oak, had come down on one side. Thea steeled herself and quickly glanced in the direction of the lake. The dock was in need of repair, too, and she tried to concentrate on that, but the expanse of blue water stretching out beyond the dock brought a sheen of sweat to her forehead. Nausea roiled in her stomach and she swallowed convulsively as she jerked her gaze back to the house and concentrated instead on the peeling paint of the front porch.

Last night, he had killed her. The expression in those aquamarine eyes had been calm and terrifyingly remote as he held her beneath the cool lake water, his arms like steel as her panicked struggles decreased in strength, until her tortured lungs had given up their last precious bit of oxygen and she had inhaled her own death.

She had awakened in the early dawn, sweating and trembling, and known that she couldn't go on like this much longer without having a nervous breakdown. She had gotten up, put on a pot of coffee, and spent the next several hours overloading on caffeine while she made her plans. She had no work going on right now, so mapping out free time for herself was easy. It probably wasn't smart, since summer was when she made the bulk of her income, but it was easy. At an hour when she could reasonably expect her parents to be awake, she'd called and asked their permission to spend a couple of weeks at the lake. As she had expected, they were delighted that she was finally going to take a vacation. Thea's brothers and their families regularly made use of the summer house, but for one reason or another, Thea hadn't been back to the lake since she was eighteen. Eleven years was a long time, but life had somehow gotten in the way. First there had been college and the need to work in the summer to finance it, then a couple of boring jobs in her chosen field that told her she had chosen the wrong field.

She had stumbled onto her career as a house-painter by accident, when she had been out of a job and desperate for anything that would bring in some money. To her surprise, despite the hot, hard work, she had liked painting houses. As time went on, more and more jobs came her way. During the winters she got some inside jobs, but she usually worked like a fiend during the summers, and simply hadn't been able to get away to join the family at any of their outings to the lake.

"But what about your birthday?" her mother asked, suddenly remembering the upcoming event. "Aren't you going to be here?"

Thea hesitated. Her family was big on birthdays. Now that her brothers were married and had children, with their wives and kids thrown into the mix, there wasn't a single month in the year when *someone's* birthday wasn't being celebrated. "I don't know," she finally said. "I'm tired, Mom. I really need a rest." That wasn't why she wanted to go to the lake, but neither was it a lie. She hadn't slept well for almost a month, and fatigue was pulling at her. "How would a delayed party sit with you?"

"Well, I suppose that would be okay," her mother said doubtfully. "I'll have to let the boys know."

"Yeah, I'd hate for them to pull a birthday prank on the wrong day," Thea replied in a dry tone. "If they've already ordered a load of chicken manure to be delivered to me, they'll just have to hold it for a few days."

Her mother chuckled. "They've never gone quite that far."

"Only because they know I'd do something twice as bad to them."

"Have fun up at the lake, honey, but be careful. I don't know if I like the idea of you being there all alone."

"I'll be careful," Thea promised. "Are there any supplies in the house?"

"I think there are a few cans of soup in the pantry, but that's about it. Check in when you get there, okay?"

"Check in" was code for what her father called Pick Up The Phone And Let Your Mother Know You're All Right So She Won't Call Missing Persons. Mrs. Marlow normally let her children get on with their lives, but when she said "check in" they all knew that she was a little anxious.

"I'll call as soon as I get to the grocery store."

Thea had kept her promise, calling in as soon as she arrived at the small grocery store where they'd always bought their supplies for the summer house. Now she sat in her car in front of the house, frozen with fear at the nearness of the lake, while bags of perishables slowly thawed in the backseat.

She forced herself to breathe deeply, beating down the fear. All right, so she couldn't look at the water. She would keep her eyes averted as she unloaded the car.

The screen door creaked as she opened it, a familiar sound that eased the strain in her expression. The screened front porch ran all the way across the front of the house, and in her childhood had been occupied by a collection of mismatched Adirondack, wicker, and lawn chairs. Her mother had often sat on the porch for hours, sewing or reading, and keeping an eye on Thea and the boys as they frolicked in the lake. The porch was bare now; the Adirondacks and wickers were long gone, and she'd heard her mother say that the lawn chairs were stored in the shed out back. Thea didn't know if she would bother to get them out; she certainly wouldn't be looking at the lake if she could help it.

No, that wasn't true. She had come up here to face the fear the dreams had caused. If that meant forcing herself to stare at the water for hours, then that's what she would do. She wouldn't let this nighttime madness rob her of a lifetime of enjoyment.

When she unlocked the front door, the heat and mustiness of a closed house hit her in the face. She wrinkled her nose and plunged inside, unlocking and opening every window to let in fresh air. By the time she had carried in the groceries and stored the perishables in the refrigerator, the light breeze had gone a long way toward sweetening the air.

Out of habit, Thea started to put her clothes in the same bedroom she'd always used, but halted as soon as she opened the door. Her old iron-frame bed had been replaced by two twin beds. The room was much tinier than she remembered. A slight frown knit her brow as she looked around. The bare wood floors were the same, but the walls were painted a different color now, and blinds covered the window, rather than the ruffled curtains she'd preferred as a young girl.

The boys' room had always had twin beds—three of them, in fact—and she checked inside to see if that still held true. It did, though the number of beds had dwindled to two. Thea sighed. She would have liked to sleep in her old room, but probably her parents' room was the only one with a double bed, and she knew she'd appreciate the comfort even more. She had a queen-size bed in her apartment.

She felt like Goldilocks as she opened the door to the third bedroom, and she burst out laughing. Sure enough, here was the bed that was just right. The double bed was no more. In its place was a king-size bed that took up the majority of the floor space, leaving only enough room on either side to maneuver while making up the bed. A long double dresser occupied most of the remaining space. She would have to be careful about stubbing her toes in here, but she would definitely sleep in comfort.

As she hung her clothes in the closet, she heard the unmistakable creak of the screen door, heavy footsteps on the porch, and then two short, hard knocks on the frame of the open front door. Startled, Thea stood very still. A cold knot of fear began to form in her stomach. She had no idea who could be at the door. She had never been afraid here before—the crime rate was so low that it was almost nonexistent—but abruptly she was terrified. What if a vagrant had watched her unload the car, and knew she was here alone? She had already checked in with her mother, to let her know she'd arrived safely, so no one would expect to hear from her for another week or so. She'd told her mother that she intended to stay about two weeks. She could be murdered or kidnapped, and it might be two weeks or longer before anyone knew she was missing.

There were other houses on the lake, of course, but none within sight. The closest one, a rental, was about half a mile away, hidden behind a finger of land that jutted into the lake. Sammy What's-his-name's family had rented it that summer when she was fourteen, she remembered. Who knew who was renting it now, or if someone hadn't bothered with renting and had simply broken in.

She hadn't heard another car or a boat, so that meant whoever was on the porch had walked. Only the rental house was within realistic walking distance. That meant he was a stranger, rather than someone belonging to the families they had met here every summer.

Her imagination had run away with her, she thought, but she couldn't control her rapid, shallow breathing, or the hard pounding of her heartbeat. All she could do was stand there in the bed-room, like a small animal paralyzed by the approach of a predator.

The front door was open. There was another screen door there, but it wasn't latched. There was nothing to stop him, whoever he was, from simply walking in.

If she was in danger, then she was trapped. She had no weapon, other than one of the kitchen knives, but she couldn't get to them without being seen. She cast an agonized glance at the window. What were her chances of getting it open and climbing out without being heard? Given the silence in the house, she realized, not very good.

That hard double knock sounded again. At least he was still on the porch.

Maybe she *was* crazy. How did she know it was even a man? By the heaviness of the footsteps? Maybe it was just a large woman.

No. It was a man. She was certain of it. Even his knocks had sounded masculine, too hard to have been made by a woman's softer hand.

"Hello? Is anyone home?"

Thea shuddered as the deep voice reverberated through the house, through her very bones. It was definitely a man's voice, and it sounded oddly familiar, even though she knew she'd never heard it before.

My God, she suddenly thought, disgusted with herself. What was wrong with her? If the man on the porch meant her any harm, cowering here in the bedroom wouldn't do her any good. And besides, a criminal would simply open the door and come on in, would already have done so. This was probably a perfectly nice man who was out for a walk and had seen a new neighbor arrive. Maybe he hadn't seen *her* at all, but noticed the car in the driveway. She was making a fool out of herself with these stupid suspicions, this panic.

Still, logic could only go so far in calming her fears. It took a lot of self-control to straighten her shoulders and forcibly regulate her breathing, and even more to force her feet to move toward the bedroom door. She stopped once more, still just out of sight, to get an even firmer grip on her courage. Then she stepped out of the bedroom into the living room, and into the view of the man on the porch.

She looked at the open door, and her heart almost failed her. He was silhouetted against the bright light beyond and she couldn't make out his features, but he was big. Six-three, at least, with shoulders that filled the doorframe. It was only her imagination, it had to be, but there seemed to be an indefinable tension in the set of those shoulders, something at once wary and menacing.

There was no way she could make herself go any closer. If he made a move to open the screen, she would bolt for the back door in the kitchen. Her purse was in the bedroom behind her and she wouldn't be able to grab it, but her car keys were in her jeans pocket, so she should be able to dive into the car and lock the doors before he could reach her, then drive for help.

She cleared her throat. "Yes?" she managed to say. "May I help you?" Despite her effort, her voice came out low and husky. To her dismay, she sounded almost . . . inviting. Maybe that was better than terrified, but she was doubtful. Which was more likely to trigger an approach by a predator, fear or a perceived sexual invitation?

Stop it! she fiercely told herself. Her visitor hadn't said or done anything to warrant this kind of paranoia.

"I'm Richard Chance," the man said, his deep

voice once again sinking through her skin, going all the way to her bones. "I'm renting the house next door for the summer. I saw your car in the driveway and stopped by to introduce myself."

Relief was almost as debilitating as terror, Thea realized as her muscles loosened and threatened to collapse altogether. She reached out an unsteady hand to brace herself against the wall.

"I—I'm glad to meet you. I'm Thea Marlow."

"Thea," he repeated softly. There was a subtle sensuality in the way he formed her name, almost as if he were tasting it. "Glad to meet you, Thea Marlow. I know you're probably still unpacking, so I won't keep you. See you tomorrow."

He turned to go, and Thea took a hasty step toward the door, then another. By the time he reached out to open the screen, she was at the doorway. "How do you know I'm still unpacking?" she blurted, tensing again.

He paused, though he didn't turn around. "Well, I take a long walk in the mornings, and your car wasn't here this morning. When I touched your car hood just now, it was still warm, so you haven't been here long. It was a reasonable assumption."

It was. Reasonable, logical. But why had he checked her car hood to see how hot it was? Suspicion kept her silent.

Then, slowly, he turned to face her. The bright sunlight glinted on the glossy darkness of his hair, thick and as lustrous as a mink's pelt, and clearly revealed every strong line of his face. His eyes met hers through the fine mesh of the screens, and a slow, unreadable smile lifted the corners of his mouth. "See you tomorrow, Thea Marlow."

Motionless again, Thea watched him walk away. Blood drained from her head and she thought she might faint. There was a buzzing in her ears, and her lips felt numb. Darkness began edging into her field of vision and she realized that she really *was* going to faint. Clumsily she dropped to her hands and knees and let her head hang forward until the dizziness began to fade.

My God. *It was him!*

There was no mistaking it. Though she'd never seen his face in her dreams, she recognized him. When he had turned to face her and those vivid aquamarine eyes had glinted at her, every cell in her body had tingled in recognition.

Richard Chance was the man in her dreams.

3

Thea was so shaken that she actually began loading all of her stuff back into the car, ready to flee back to White Plains and the dubious safety of her own apartment. In the end, though still trembling with reaction, she returned her supplies and clothes to the house and then resorted to her own time-honored remedy of coffee. What good would going home do? The problem was the dreams, which had her so on edge that she had panicked when a neighbor came to call and then had immediately decided, on the basis of his vivid eye color, that he was the man in her dreams.

Okay, time for a reality check, she sternly told

herself as she nursed her third cup of coffee. She had never been able to see Marcus-Neill-Duncan's face, because of the damn mist that always seemed to be between them. All she had been able to tell was that he had long, dark hair and aquamarine eyes. On the other hand, she knew his smell, his touch, every inch of his muscled body, the power with which he made love. What was she supposed to do, ask Richard Chance to strip down so she could inspect him for similarities?

A lot of people in the world had dark hair; most of them, as a matter of fact. A lot of dark-haired men had vivid eyes. It was merely chance that she had happened to meet Richard Chance at a time when she wasn't exactly logical on the subject of eye color. She winced at the play on words, and got up to pour her fourth cup of coffee.

She had come here with a purpose. She refused to let a dream, no matter how disturbing and realistic, destroy her enjoyment of something she had always loved. It wasn't just this new fear of water that she hated, but what the dreams were doing to her memories of the summers of her childhood. Losing that joy would be like losing the center of her being. Damn it, she *would* learn to love the water again. Maybe she couldn't look at the lake just yet, but by the time she left here, she swore, she would be swimming in it again. She couldn't let her stupid paranoia about Richard Chance frighten her away.

It didn't mean anything that he had said her name as if savoring it. Actually, it did mean something, but that something was connected to his sexual organs rather than to her dreams. Thea knew she wasn't a raving beauty, but neither was she blind to her attractiveness to men. She was often dissatisfied with her mop of thick, curly, chestnut hair, despairing of ever taming it into any discernible style, but men, for reasons of their own, liked it. Her eyes were green, her features even and clean-cut, and the rigors of her job kept her lean and in shape. Now that her nerves were settling down, she realized that the gleam in those memorable eyes had been interested rather than threatening.

That could be difficult, considering that she had come up here to work through some problems rather than indulge in a summer fling with a new neighbor. She wasn't in the mood for romance, even of the casual, two-week variety. She would be cool and uninterested in any invitations he might extend, he would get the hint, and that would be that.

"COME."

She turned, and saw him standing under the willow tree, his hand outstretched. She didn't want to go to him, every instinct shouted for her to run, but the compulsion to obey was a terrible need inside her, an ache and a hunger that he could satisfy.

"Come," he said again, and her unwilling feet began moving her across the cool, dewy grass. Her white night-dress swirled around her legs, and she felt her nakedness beneath the thin fabric. No matter how many layers of clothing covered her, he always made her feel unclothed and vulnerable. She knew she shouldn't be out here alone, especially with him, but she couldn't make herself go back inside. She knew he was a dangerous man, and it didn't matter. All that mattered was being with him; the propriety that had ruled her life suddenly meant less to her than did the wet grass beneath her bare feet.

When she reached him, they stood facing each other like adversaries, neither moving nor speaking for a long moment that stretched out until she thought she would scream from the tension of it. Like the predator he was, he had been stalking her for weeks, and now he sensed, with unerring instinct, that she was within his grasp. He put his hand on her arm, his touch burning with vitality, and a smile lightly touched his hard mouth as he felt her betraying quiver. "Do you think I will hurt you?" he asked, his amusement evident.

She shivered again. "Yes," she said, looking up at him. "In one way or another . . . yes."

Inexorably he drew her closer, until her flimsily clad body rested against him and the animal heat of his flesh dispelled the chill of the night air. Automatically she put her hands up to rest against his chest, and the feel of the rock-hard sheets of muscle made her breath catch. No other man she'd ever touched was as hard and vital as this—this warrior, whose life was based on death and destruction. She wanted to deny him, to turn away from him, but was as helpless as a leaf on the wind to defy the currents that swept her toward him.

He brushed his lips against her hair in an oddly tender gesture, one she hadn't expected from such a man. "Then lie down with me," he murmured, "and I'll show you the sweetest pain of all."

Thea awoke, the echoes of her own cries still lingering in the darkness of the bedroom. He had; oh, he had. She was lying on her back, her nightgown twisted around her waist, her legs open and her knees raised. The last remnants of completion still throbbed delicately in her loins.

She put her hands over her face and burst into tears.

It was more than disturbing—it was humiliating. The damn man not only took over her dreams, he dominated her body as well. Her entire sense of self was grounded in her sturdy normality, her good common sense. Thea had always thought of herself as *dependable*, and suddenly that description no longer seemed to apply. Because of the dreams, she had taken a two-week vacation right in the middle of her busiest time, which wasn't dependable. What was going on with her now defied common sense, defied all her efforts to understand what was happening. And it certainly wasn't *normal* to have frighteningly intense climaxes night after night, while sleeping alone.

Choking back her tears, she stumbled out of bed and down the hall to the bathroom, where she stood under the shower and tried to rid her body of the sensation of being touched by invisible hands. When she felt marginally calmer, she dried off and relocated to the kitchen, where she put on fresh coffee and then sat drinking it and watching the dawn progress into a radiantly sunny morning.

The kitchen was located at the back of the house, so the lake wasn't visible from the window, and Thea slowly relaxed as she watched tiny birds flitting from branch to branch in a nearby tree, twittering to each other and doing bird things.

She had to stop letting these dreams upset her so much. No matter how disturbing their content, they were still just dreams. When she looked at this rationally, the only thing about the dreams that had really affected her life was the unreasoning fear of water they had caused. She had come to the lake to work through that fear, to force herself to face it, and if she could overcome that she would be satisfied. Maybe it wasn't normal to have such sexually intense dreams, or for the same man who brought her such pleasure to kill her in some of those dreams, but she would handle it. Who knew what had triggered the dreams? They could have been triggered by her eclectic reading material, or some movie she'd watched, or a combination of both. Probably they would cease as mysteriously as they had appeared.

In the meantime, she had already wasted one

day of her self-prescribed recovery period. Except for that one nauseating glance at the lake when she had first arrived, she had managed to completely ignore the water.

All right, Theadora, she silently scolded herself. *Stop being such a wuss. Get off your can and do what you came here to do.*

In an unconscious gesture of preparation, she ran her fingers through her hair, which had almost dried in the time she had spent drinking coffee and postponing the inevitable. She could feel the unruly curls, thick and vibrant, taking shape under her fingers. She probably looked a fright, she thought, and was glad there was no one there to see. For this entire two weeks, she could largely ignore her appearance except for basic cleanliness, and she looked forward to the freedom.

For comfort, she poured one final cup of coffee and carried it with her out onto the porch, carefully keeping her gaze cast downward so she wouldn't spill the hot liquid. Yeah, she thought wryly, that was a great excuse to keep from seeing the lake first thing when she opened the door.

She kept her eyes downcast as she opened the front door and felt the cool morning air wash over her bare feet. She had simply pulled on her night-gown again after leaving the shower, and the thin material was no match for the chill that the sun hadn't quite dispelled.

All right. Time to do it. Firmly gripping the cup like a lifeline, she slowly raised her eyes so that her gaze slid first across the floor of the porch, then onto the overgrown grass, and then down the slight slope toward the lake. She deliberately con-centrated on only a narrow field of vision, so that everything else was blurred. There was the willow tree off to the left, and—

He was standing beneath the spreading limbs, just as he had in her dream.

Thea's heart almost stopped. Dear God, now her dreams had started manifesting themselves during her waking hours, in the form of hallucina-tions. She tried to blink, tried to banish the vision, but all she could do was stare in frozen horror at the man standing as motionless as a statue, his aquamarine eyes shining across the distance.

Then he moved, and she jerked in reaction as she simultaneously realized two things, each as disturbing in a different way as the other.

One, the "vision" was Richard Chance. The figure under the tree was a real human being, not a figment of her imagination.

Two, she hadn't realized it before, but last night she had been able to see her dream lover's face for the first time, and it had been Richard Chance's face.

She calmed her racing heartbeat. Of course her subconscious had chosen his features for those of the dream lover; after all, she had been startled that very day by the similarity of their eyes. This quirk of her dreams, at least, was logical.

They faced each other across the dewy grass, and a slow smile touched the hard line of his mouth, almost causing her heartbeat to start galloping again. For the sake of her circuits, she hoped he wouldn't smile too often.

Then Richard Chance held out his hand to her, and said, "Come."

4

What little color she had, drained from Thea's face. "What did you say?" she whispered.

He couldn't possibly have heard her. He was standing a good thirty yards away; she had barely been able to hear the one word he'd spoken, though somehow the sound had been perfectly clear, as if she had heard it inside herself as well as out. But the expression on his face changed subtly, to something more alert, his eyes more piercing. His outstretched hand suddenly seemed more imperious, though his tone became cajoling. "Thea. Come with me."

Shakily she stepped back, intending to close

the door. This had to be pure chance, but it was spooky.

"Don't run," he said softly. "There's no need to. I won't hurt you."

Thea had never considered herself a coward. Her brothers would have described her as being a touch too foolhardy for her own good, stubbornly determined to climb any tree they could climb, or to swing out on a rope as high as they did before dropping into the lake. Despite the eerie similarity between the dream and what he'd just now said, her spine stiffened, and she stared at Richard Chance as he stood under the willow tree, surrounded by a slight mist. Once again, she was letting a weird coincidence spook her, and she was tired of being afraid. She knew instinctively that the best way to conquer any fear was to face it— hence her trip to the lake—so she decided to take a good, hard look at Mr. Chance to catalog the similarities between him and her dream lover. She looked, and almost wished she hadn't.

The resemblance wasn't just in his eyes and the color of his hair. She could see it now in the powerful lines of his body, so tall and rugged. He was wearing jeans and hiking boots and a short-sleeved chambray shirt that revealed the muscularity of his arms. She noticed the thickness of his wrists, the wrists of a man who regularly did hard physical work . . . *the wrists of a swordsman.*

She gasped, shaken by the thought. Where had it come from? What did she know about swordsmen? They weren't exactly thick on the ground; she'd never even met anyone who fenced. And even as she pictured the elegant moves of fencing, she discarded that comparison. No, by *swordsman* she meant someone who used a heavy broadsword in battle, slashing and hacking. A flash of memory darted through her, and she saw Richard Chance with a huge claymore in his hand, only he had called himself Neill . . . and then he was Marcus, and it was the short Roman sword he wielded—

No. She couldn't let herself think like that. The dreams were a subconscious fantasy, nothing more. She didn't really recognize anything about Richard Chance. She had simply met him at a time when she was emotionally vulnerable and off-balance, almost as if she were on the rebound from a failed romance. She had to get a grip, because there was no way this man had anything to do with her dreams.

He was still standing there, his hand out-stretched as if only a second had gone by, rather than the full minute it felt like.

And then he smiled again, those vivid eyes crinkling at the corners. "Don't you want to see the baby turtles?" he asked.

Baby turtles. The prospect was disarming, and surprisingly charmed by the idea, somehow Thea found herself taking a couple of steps forward, until she was standing at the screen door to the porch. Only then did she stop and look down at her nightgown. "I need to change clothes."

His gaze swept down her. "You look great to me." He didn't try to disguise the huskiness of appreciation in his tone. "Besides, they might be gone if you don't come now."

Thea chewed her lip. The nightgown wasn't a racy number, after all; it was plain white cotton, with a modest neckline and little cap sleeves, and the hem reached her ankles. Caution warred with her desire to see the turtles. Suddenly she couldn't think of anything cuter than baby turtles. Making a quick decision, she pushed open the door and stepped out into the tall grass. She had to lift her nightgown hem to midcalf to keep it from dragging in the dew and getting wet. Carefully she picked her way across the overgrown yard to the tall man waiting for her.

She had almost reached him when she realized how close she was to the water.

She froze in midstep, unable to even glance to the right where the lake murmured so close to her feet. Instead, her panic-stricken gaze locked on his face, instinctively begging him for help.

He straightened, every muscle in his body tightening as he became alert in response to her reaction. His eyes narrowed, and his gaze swung sharply from side to side, looking for whatever had frightened her. "What is it?" he rasped as he caught her forearm and protectively pulled her nearer, into the heat and shelter of his body.

Thea shivered and opened her mouth to tell him, but the closeness of his body, at once comforting and alarming, confused her so she couldn't think what to say. She didn't know which alarmed her more, her nearness to the lake or her nearness to him. She had always loved the lake, and was very wary of him, but his automatic response to her distress jolted something inside her, and suddenly she wanted to press herself against him. The warm scent of his skin filled her nostrils, her lungs—a heady combination of soap, fresh air, clean sweat, and male muskiness. He had pulled her against his left side, leaving his right arm free, and she could feel the reassuring steadiness of his heartbeat thudding within the strong wall of his chest.

She was abruptly, acutely aware of her naked-ness beneath the nightgown. Her breasts throbbed where they pressed against his side, and her thighs began trembling. My God, what was she doing out here, dressed like this? What had happened to her much-vaunted common sense? Since the dreams had begun, she didn't seem to have any sense at all. No way should she be this close to a man she'd just met the day before. She knew she should pull away from him, but from the moment he'd touched her she had felt an odd sense of intimacy, of *rightness*, as if she had merely returned to a place she'd been many times before.

His free hand threaded through her damp curls. "Thea?" he prompted, some of the alertness relaxing from his muscles. "Did something scare you?"

She cleared her throat and fought off a wave of

dizziness. His hand in her hair felt so familiar, as if . . . She jerked her wayward thoughts from that impossible path. "The water," she finally said, her voice still tight with fear. "I—I'm afraid of the water, and I just noticed how close I was to the bank."

"Ah," he said in a slow sound of realization. "That's understandable. But how were you going to see the turtles if you're afraid of the water?"

Dismayed, she looked up at him. "I didn't think about that." How could she tell him that her fear of the water was so recent that she wasn't used to thinking in terms of what she could or couldn't do based on the proximity of water. Her attention splintered again, caught by the angle of his jaw when viewed from below. It was a very strong jaw, she noticed, with a stubborn chin. He had a fairly heavy beard; despite the evident fact that he had just shaved, she could see the dark whiskers that would give him a heavy five-o'clock shadow. Again that nagging sense of familiarity touched her, and she wanted to put her hand to his face. She wondered if he was always consider-ate enough to shave before making love, and had a sudden powerful image of that stubbled chin being gently rubbed against the curve of her breast.

She gave a startled jerk, a small motion that he controlled almost before it began, his arm tightening around her and pulling her even more solidly against him. "The turtles are just over here, about fifty feet," he murmured, bending his head down so that his jaw just brushed her curls. "Could you look at them if I stay between you and the lake, and hold you so you know you won't fall in?"

Oh, he was good. She noticed it in a peripheral kind of way. Whenever he did something she might find alarming—something that *should* alarm her, like take her in his arms—he immediately distracted her with a diverting comment. She saw the ploy, but . . . baby turtles were so cute. She thought about his proposition. It was probably a dangerous illusion, but she felt safe in his arms, warmed by his heat and wrapped up in all that muscled power. Desire began in that moment, a delicate, delicious unfurling deep inside her . . . or maybe it had begun before, at his first touch, and had just now grown strong enough for her to recognize it. Why else had she thought about the roughness of his chin against her body? She knew she should go back inside. She had already made the logical decision that she had no time for even lightweight romance. But logic had nothing to do with the wild mixture of reactions she had felt since first seeing this man, fear, panic, compulsion and desire all swirling together so she never knew from one minute to the next how she was going to react. She didn't like it, didn't like anything about it. She wanted to be the old Thea again, not this nervous, illogical creature she didn't recognize.

All right, so throw logic out the window. It hadn't done her much good since the dreams had begun anyway. She looked up into watchful aquamarine eyes and threw caution to the dogs, too, deciding instead to operate on pure instinct. "Maybe that would work. Let's try it."

She thought she saw a flare of triumph in those crystalline eyes, but when she looked more closely she saw only a certain male pleasure. "Let's go a couple of steps farther away from the water," he suggested, already steering her along with that solid arm around her waist. "We'll still be able to see the turtles. Tell me if we're still too close, okay? I don't want you to be nervous."

She chuckled, and was surprised at herself for

being able to laugh. How could she not be nervous? She was too close to the water, and way too close to him. "If I were wearing shoes, I'd be shaking in them," she admitted.

He glanced down at her bare feet, and the way she was having to hold up her nightgown to keep it out of the wet grass. "There might be briers," he said by way of explanation as he bent down and hooked his other arm beneath her knees. Thea gave a little cry of surprise as he lifted her, grabbing at his shirt in an effort to steady herself. He grinned as he settled her high against his chest. "How's this?"

Frightening. Exciting. Her heart was thudding wildly, and that first pressure of desire was becoming more intense. She cast a look at the ground and said, "High."

"Are you afraid of heights, too?"

"No, just of water." *And of you, big guy*. But far more attracted than afraid, she realized.

He carried her along the bank, taking care not to get any closer to the water, while Thea looked everywhere but at the lake. The most convenient point of focus was his throat, strong and brown, with a small vulnerable hollow beneath the solid knot of his Adam's apple. The close proximity of his bare skin made her lips tingle, as if she had just pressed them into that little hollow where his pulse throbbed so invitingly.

"We have to be quiet," he whispered, and eased the last few steps. They had left the relative neatness of the overgrown yard and were in a tangle of bushes and weeds that probably did contain briers. Given her bare feet, she was just as glad he was carrying her. The trees grew more thickly here, greatly limiting the view of the lake. "They're still here, on a fallen log lying at the edge of the water. Don't make any sudden moves. I'm going to let you down, very slowly. Put your feet on my boots."

Before she could ask why, now that she was perfectly comfortable in his arms, he withdrew his arm from beneath her legs and let her lower body slide downward. Though he took care not to let her nightgown get caught between them, the friction of her body moving over his could scarcely have been more enticing. She caught her breath, her breasts and thighs tingling with heat even as she sought his boot tops with her feet and let her weight come to rest on them. Nor was he unaffected; there was no mistaking the firm swelling in his groin.

He seemed more capable than she of ignoring it, however. He had both arms around her, holding her snugly against him, but his head was turned toward the lake. She could feel excitement humming through him, but it didn't seem to be sexual in nature, despite his semierection.

"There are seven of them," he whispered, his voice the husky murmur of a lover. "They're lined up on the log like silver-dollar pancakes with legs. Just turn your head and take a peek, and I'll hold you steady so you'll feel safe."

Thea hesitated, torn between her desire to see the little turtles and her fear of the water. Her hands were clutching his upper arms, and she could feel the hard biceps flex as he held her a little closer. "Take your time," he said, still whispering, and she felt his lips brush her curls.

She took a deep breath and steeled herself. Half a second later she convulsively buried her face against his chest, shaking, trying to fight back the rise of nausea. He cuddled her, comforting her with a slight rocking motion of his body while he murmured reassuring noises that weren't really words.

Two minutes later she tried again, with much the same result.

By the fourth try, tears of frustration were welling in her eyes. Richard tried to take her back to the house, but the stubbornness her brothers were well acquainted with came to the fore, and she refused to leave. By God, she was going to see those turtles.

Ten minutes later, she still hadn't managed more than a single peek before the panic and nausea would hit her, and she was getting furious with herself. The turtles were happily sunning themselves right now, but they could be gone in the next second.

"I'm going to do it this time," she announced, her tone one of angry determination.

Richard sighed. "All right." She was well aware that he could simply pick her up and stride away at any time, but somehow she sensed that he would stand there until she was ready to give up the effort. She braced herself and began to turn her head by slow degrees. "While you're torturing yourself, I'll pass the time by remembering how I could see through your nightgown when you were walking across the yard," he said.

Stunned, Thea found herself blinking at the little turtles for two full seconds while she reeled under the impact of what he'd just said. When her head jerked back around, there was more outrage than panic in the motion. *"What?"*

"I could see through your nightgown," he repeated helpfully. A smile tugged at his mouth, and his crystalline eyes revealed even more amusement as he looked down at her. "The sun was shining at an angle. I saw . . ." He let the sentence trail off.

She pushed at his arms in an effort to loosen them, without results. "Just what *did* you see?"

"Everything." He seemed to enjoy the memory. He made a little humming sound of pleasure in his throat. "You have gorgeous little nipples."

Thea flushed brightly, even as she felt the aforementioned gorgeous little nipples tighten into hard buds. The reaction was matched by one in his pants.

"Look at the turtles," he said.

Distracted, she did just that. At the same time he stroked his right hand down her bottom, the touch searing her flesh through the thin fabric, and cupped and lifted her so that the notch of her thighs settled over the hard bulge beneath his fly. Thea's breath caught in her lungs. She stared blindly at the turtles, but her attention was on the apex of her thighs. She bit back a moan, and barely restrained the urge to rock herself against that bulge. She could feel herself alter inside, muscles tightening and loosening, growing moist as desire built to a strong throb.

He was a stranger. She had to be out of her mind to stand here with him in such a provocative position. But though her mind knew he was a stranger, her body accepted him as if she had known him forever. The resulting conflict rendered her all but incapable of action.

The little turtles were indeed the size of silver-dollar pancakes, with tiny reptilian heads and stubby legs. They were lined up on the half-submerged log, the water gently lapping just below them. Thea stared at the sheen of water for several seconds before she realized what she was doing, so successfully had he distracted her.

"Richard," she breathed.

"H'mmm?" His voice was deeper, his breathing slightly faster.

"I'm looking at the turtles."

"I know, sweetheart. I knew you could do it."

"I wouldn't want to go any closer, but I'm looking at the water."

"That's good." He paused. "As you learn to trust me, you'll gradually get over your fear."

What a strange thing to say, she thought. What did he have to do with her fear of the water? That was caused by the dreams, not him. She wanted to ask him what he meant, but it was difficult to think straight when he was holding her so intimately, and when his erection was thrusting against her more insistently with each passing moment.

Then something unseen alarmed the little turtles, or perhaps one of them simply decided he'd had enough sun and the others followed suit, but all at once they slid off the log and plopped into the water, one by one, the entire action taking place so fast that it was over in a second. Ripples spread out from the log, resurrecting an echo of nausea in Thea's stomach. She swallowed and looked away, and the sensual spell was broken.

He knew it, too. Before she could speak, he matter-of-factly lifted her in his arms and carried her back to the yard.

Remembering what he'd said about her nightgown, she blushed hotly again as soon as he set her on her feet. He glanced at her hot cheeks, and amusement gleamed in his eyes.

"Don't laugh," she muttered crossly as she moved away from him. Though it was probably way too late, she tried for dignity. "Thank you for showing me the turtles, and for being so patient with me."

"You're welcome," he said in a grave tone that still managed to convey his hidden laughter.

She scowled. She didn't know whether to back away or to turn around and let him get a good view of her rear end, too. She didn't have enough hands to cover all her points of interest, and it was too late anyway. She compromised by sidling.

"Thea."

She paused, her brows lifted in question.

"Will you come on a picnic with me this afternoon?"

A picnic? She stared at him, wondering once again at the disturbing blend of strangeness and familiarity she felt about him. Like the baby turtles, a picnic sounded almost unbearably tempting; this whole thing was feeling as if she had opened a book so compelling that she couldn't

LINDA HOWARD

stop turning page after page. Still, she felt herself pulling back. "I don't—"

"There's a tree in a fallow field about a mile from here," he interrupted, and all amusement had left his ocean-colored eyes. "It's huge, with limbs bigger around than my waist. It looks as if it's been here forever. I'd like to lie on a blanket spread in its shade, put my head in your lap, and tell you about my dreams."

5

Thea wanted to run. Damn courage; discretion demanded that she flee. She wanted to, but her legs wouldn't move. Her whole body seemed to go numb. She let the hem of her nightgown drop into the wet grass, and she stared dumbly at him. "Who are you?" she finally whispered.

He studied the sudden terror in her eyes, and regret flashed across his face. "I told you," he finally answered, his tone mild. "Richard Chance."

"What—what did you mean about your dreams?"

Again he paused, his sharp gaze still fastened on her so that not even the smallest nuance of expression could escape him. "Let's go inside," he suggested, approaching to gently take her arm and guide her stumbling steps toward the house. "We'll talk there."

Thea stiffened her trembling legs and dug in her heels, dragging him to a stop. Or rather, he allowed her to do so. She had never before in her life been as aware of a man's strength as she was of his. He wasn't a muscle-bound hulk, but the steeliness of his body was evident. "What about your dreams?" she asked insistently. "What do you want?"

He sighed, and released his grip to lightly rub his fingers up and down the tender underside of her arm. "What I don't want is for you to be frightened," he replied. "I've just found you, Thea. The last thing I want is to scare you away."

His tone was quiet and sincere, and worked a strange kind of magic on her. How could a woman fail to be, if not reassured, at least calmed by the very evenness of his words? Her alarm faded somewhat, and Thea found herself being shepherded once again toward the house. This time she didn't try to stop him. At least she could change into something more suitable before they had this talk on which he was so insistent.

She pulled away from him as soon as they were inside, and gathered her tattered composure around herself like a cloak. "The kitchen is there," she said, pointing. "If you'll put on a fresh pot of coffee, I'll be with you as soon as I get dressed."

He gave her another of his open looks of pure male appreciation, his gaze sliding over her from head to foot. "Don't bother on my account," he murmured.

"Your account is exactly why I'm bothering," she retorted, and his quick grin sent butterflies on a giddy flight in her stomach. Despite her best efforts, she was warmed by his unabashed attraction. "The coffee's in the cupboard to the left of the sink."

"Yes, ma'am." He winked and ambled toward the kitchen. Thea escaped into the bedroom and closed the door, leaning against it in relief. Her legs were still trembling. What was going on? She felt as if she had tumbled down the rabbit hole. He was a stranger, she had met him only the day before, and yet there were moments, more and more of them, when she felt as if she knew him as well as she knew herself, times when his voice reverberated deep inside of her like an internal bell. Her body responded to him as it never had to anyone else, with an ease that was as if they had been lovers for years.

He said and did things that eerily echoed her dreams. But how could she have dreamed about a man whom she hadn't met? This was totally outside her experience; she had no explanation for it, unless she had suddenly become clairvoyant.

Yeah, sure. Thea shook her head as she stripped out of the nightgown and opened a dresser drawer to get out bra and panties. She could just hear her brothers if she were to dare mention such a thing to them. "Woo, woo," they'd hoot, snorting with laughter. "Somebody find a turban for her to wear! Madam Theadora's going to tell our fortunes."

She pulled on jeans and a T-shirt and stuck her feet into a pair of sneakers. Comforted by the armor of clothing, she felt better prepared to face Richard Chance again. It was a loony idea to think she'd met him in her dreams, but she knew one sure way of finding out. In every incarnation, her dream warrior's left thigh had been scarred, a long, jagged red line that ended just a few inches above his knee. All she had to do was ask him to drop his pants so she could see his leg, and she'd settle this mystery once and for all.

Right. She could just see herself handing him a cup of coffee: "Do you take cream or sugar? Would you like a cinnamon roll? Would you please remove your pants?"

Her breasts tingled and her stomach muscles tightened. The prospect of seeing him nude was more tempting than it should have been. There was something dangerously appealing in the thought of asking him to remove his clothing. He would do it, too, those vivid eyes glittering at her all the while. He was as aware as she that, if they were caught, he would be killed—

Thea jerked herself out of the disturbing fantasy. *Killed?* Why on earth had she thought that? It was probably just the dreams again—but she had never dreamed that *he* had been killed, only herself. And he had been the killer.

Her stomach muscles tightened again, but this time with the return of that gut-level fear she'd felt from the moment she'd heard his step on the porch. She had feared him even before she'd met him. He was a man whose reputation preceded him—

Stop it! Thea fiercely admonished herself. What

reputation? She'd never heard of Richard Chance. She looked around the bedroom, seeking to ground herself in the very normality of her surroundings. She felt as if things were blurring, but the outlines of the furniture were reassuringly sharp. No, the blurring was inside, and she was quietly terrified. She was truly slipping over that fine line between reality and dreamworld.

Maybe Richard Chance didn't exist. Maybe he was merely a figment of her imagination, brought to life by those thrice-damned dreams.

But the alluring scent of fresh coffee was no dream. Thea slipped out of the bedroom and crossed the living room to stand unnoticed in the doorway to the kitchen. Or she should have been unnoticed, because her sneakered feet hadn't made any noise. But Richard Chance, standing with the refrigerator door open while he peered at the contents, turned immediately to smile at her, and that unnerving aquamarine gaze slid over her jean-clad legs with just as much appreciation as when she'd worn only the nightgown. It didn't matter to him what she wore; he saw the female flesh, not the casing, Thea realized, as her body tightened again in automatic response to that warmly sexual survey.

"Are you real?" she asked, the faint words slipping out without plan. "Am I crazy?" Her fingers tightened into fists as she waited for his answer.

He closed the refrigerator door and quickly crossed to her, taking one of her tightly knotted fists in his much bigger hand and lifting it to his lips. "Of course you're not crazy," he reassured her. His warm mouth pressed tenderly to each white knuckle, easing the tension from her hand. "Things are happening too fast and you're a little disoriented. That's all."

The explanation, she realized, was another of his ambiguous but strangely comforting statements. And if he was a figment of her imagination, he was a very solid one, all muscle and body heat, complete with the subtle scent of his skin.

She gave him a long, considering look. "But if I am crazy," she said reasonably, "then you don't exist, so why should I believe anything you say?"

He threw back his head with a crack of laughter. "Trust me, Thea. You aren't crazy, and you aren't dreaming."

Trust me. The words echoed in her mind and her face froze, a chill running down her back as she stared up at him. Trust me. He'd said that to her before. She hadn't remembered until just now, but he'd said that to her in her dreams—the dreams in which he had killed her.

He saw her expression change, and his own expression became guarded. He turned away and poured two cups of coffee, placing them on the table before guiding her into one of the chairs. He sat down across from her and cradled a cup in both hands, inhaling the rich aroma of the steam.

He hadn't asked her how she liked her coffee, Thea noticed. Nor had she offered cream or sugar to him. He drank coffee the same way he did tea: black.

How did she even know he drank tea? A faint dizziness assailed her, and she gripped the edge of the table as she stared at him. It was the oddest sensation, as if she were sensing multiple images while her eyes saw only one. And for the first time she was conscious of a sense of incompletion, as if part of herself was missing.

She wrapped her hands around the hot cup in front of her, but didn't drink. Instead she eyed him warily. "All right, Mr. Chance, cards on the table. What about your dreams?"

He smiled and started to say something, but

then reconsidered, and his smile turned rueful. Finally he shrugged, as if he saw no point in further evasion. "I've been dreaming about you for almost a month."

She had expected it, and yet hearing him admit it was still a shock. Her hands trembled a bit. "I—I've been dreaming about you, too," she confessed. "What's happening? Do we have some sort of psychic link? I don't even believe in stuff like that!"

He sipped his coffee, watching her over the rim of the cup. "What do you believe in, Thea? Fate? Chance? Coincidence?"

"All of that, I think," she said slowly. "I think some things are meant to be . . . and some things just happen."

"How do you categorize us? Did this just happen, or are we meant to be?"

"You're assuming that there is an 'us,' " she pointed out. "We've been having weird dreams, but that isn't . . ."

"Intimate?" he suggested, his gaze sharpening.

The dreams had certainly been that. Her cheeks pinkened as she recalled some of the sexually graphic details. She hoped his dreams hadn't been mirrors of hers . . . but they had, she realized, seeing the knowledge in his eyes. Her face turned even hotter.

He burst out laughing. "If you could see your expression!"

"Stop it," she said crossly, fixing her gaze firmly on her cup because she was too embarrassed to look at him. She didn't know if she would ever be able to face him again.

"Thea, darling." His tone was patient, and achingly tender as he tried to soothe her. "I've made love to you in every way a man can love a woman . . . but only in my dreams. How can a dream possibly match reality?"

If reality was any more intense than the dreams, she thought, it would surely kill her. She traced a pattern on the tabletop with her finger, stalling while she tried to compose herself. Just how real *were* the dreams? How could he call her "darling" with such ease, and why did it sound so right to her ears? She tried to remind herself that it had been less than twenty-four hours since she had seen him for the first time, but found that the length of time meant less than nothing. There was a bone-deep recognition between them that had nothing to do with how many times the sun had risen and set.

She still couldn't look at him, but she didn't have to see him for every cell in her body to be vibrantly aware of him. The only other times she had felt so painfully alive and sensitive to another's presence were in her dreams of this man. She didn't know how, or why, their dreams had become linked, but the evidence was too overwhelming for her to deny that it had happened. But just how closely did the dreams match reality? She cleared her throat. "I know this is a strange question . . . but do you have a scar on your left thigh?"

He was silent for several moments, but finally she heard him sigh. "Yes."

She closed her eyes as the shock of his answer rolled through her. If the dreams were that accurate, then she had another question for him, and this one was far more important. She braced herself and asked it, her voice choking over the words. "In your dreams, have you killed me?"

Again he was silent, so long that finally she couldn't bear the pressure and glanced up at him. He was watching her, his gaze steady. "Yes," he said.

6

Thea shoved away from the table and bolted for the front door. He caught her there, simply wrapping his arms around her from behind and holding her locked to him. "My God, don't be afraid of me," he whispered into her tousled curls, his voice rough with emotion. "I would never hurt you. Trust me."

"Trust you!" she echoed incredulously, near tears as she struggled against his grip. "Trust *you?* How can I? How could I ever?"

"You're right about that, at least," he said, a hard tone edging into the words. "You've lowered yourself to let me touch you, give you pleasure, but you've never trusted me to love you."

She laughed wildly, with building hysteria. "I just met you yesterday! You're crazy—we're both crazy. None of this makes any sense." She clawed at his hands, trying to loosen his grasp. He simply adjusted his hold, catching her hands and linking his fingers through hers so she couldn't do any damage, and still keeping his arms wrapped around her. She was so effectively subdued that all she could do was kick at his shins, but as she was wearing sneakers and he had on boots, she doubted she was causing him much discomfort. But even knowing it was useless, she writhed and bucked against his superior strength until she had exhausted herself. Panting, unable to sustain the effort another second, she let her trembling muscles go limp.

Instantly he cuddled her closer, bending his head to brush his mouth against her temple. He kept his lips pressed there, feeling her pulse beating through the fragile skin. "It wasn't just yesterday that we met," he muttered. "It was a lifetime ago—several lifetimes. I've been here waiting for you. I knew you would come."

His touch worked an insidious magic on her; it always had. The present was blurring, mixing with the past so that she wasn't certain what was happening now and what had happened before. Just so had he held her that night when he had slipped through the camp of her father's army and sneaked into her bedchamber. Terror had beaten through her like the wings of a vulture, but she had been as helpless then as she was now. He had gagged her, and carried her silently through the night to his own camp, where he'd held her hostage against her father's attack.

She had been a virgin when he'd kidnapped her. When he had returned her, a month later, she had no longer been untouched. And she had been so stupidly in love with her erstwhile captor that she had lied to protect him, and ultimately betrayed her father.

Thea's head fell back against his shoulder. "I don't know what's happening," she murmured, and the words sounded thick, her voice drugged. The scenes that were in her head couldn't possibly be memories.

His lips sought the small hollow below her ear. "We've found each other again. Thea." As he had the first time, he said her name as if tasting it. "Thea. I like this name best of all."

"It's—it's Theadora." She had always wondered why her parents had given her such an old-fashioned, unusual name, but when she'd asked, her mother had only said, rather bemusedly, that they had simply liked it. Thea's brothers, on the other hand, had the perfectly comfortable names of Lee and Jason.

"Ah. I like that even better." He nipped her earlobe, his sharp teeth gently tugging.

"Who was I before?" she heard herself ask, then hurriedly shook her head. "Never mind. I don't believe any of this."

"Of course you do," he chided, and delicately licked the exposed, vulnerable cord of her arched neck. He was aroused again, she noticed, or maybe he'd never settled down to begin with. His hard length nestled against her jean-clad bottom. No other man had ever responded to her with such blatant desire, had wanted her so strongly and incessantly. *All she had to do was move her hips against him in that little teasing roll that always maddened him with lust, and he would take her now, pushing her against the castle wall and lifting her skirts—*

Thea jerked her drifting mind from the waking dream, but reality was scarcely less provocative, or precarious. "I don't know what's real anymore," she cried.

"We are, Thea. We're real. I know you're confused. As soon as I saw you, I knew you'd just begun remembering. I wanted to hold you, but I knew it was too soon, I knew you were frightened by what's been happening. Let's drink our coffee, and I'll answer any questions you have."

Cautiously he released her, leaving Thea feeling oddly cold and abandoned. She turned to face him, looking up at the strong bones of his features, the intense watchfulness of his vivid eyes. She felt his hunger emanating from him like a force field, enwrapping her in a primal warmth that counteracted the chill of no longer being in his arms. Another memory assailed her, of another time when she had stood and looked into his face, and seen the desire so plainly in his eyes. At that time she had been shocked and frightened, an innocent, sheltered young lady who had suddenly been thrust into harsh conditions, and she'd had only his dubious protection from danger. Dubious not because of any lack of competence, but because she thought she might be in greater danger from him than from any outside threat.

Thea drew in a slow, deep breath, feeling again that internal blurring as past and present merged, and abruptly she knew how futile it was to keep fighting the truth. As unbelievable as it was, she had to accept what was happening. She had spent her entire life—this life, anyway—secure in a tiny time frame, unaware of anything else, but now the blinders were gone and she was seeing far too much. The sheer enormity of it overwhelmed her, asked her to cast aside the comfortable boundaries of her life and step into danger, for that was what Richard Chance had brought with him when he had entered her life again. She had loved him in all his incarnations, no matter how she had struggled against him. And he had desired her, violently, arrogantly ignoring danger to come to her again and again. But for all his desire, she thought painfully, in the end he had always destroyed her. Her dreams had been warnings, acquainting her with the past so she would know to avoid him in the present.

Go. That was all she had to do, simply pack and go. Instead she let him lead her back to the kitchen, where their cups sat with coffee still gently steaming. She was disconcerted to realize how little time had passed since she had fled the table.

"How did you know where to find me?" she asked abruptly, taking a fortifying sip of coffee. "How long have you known about me?"

He gave her a considering look, as if gauging her willingness to accept his answers, and settled into the chair across from her. "To answer your second question first, I've known about you for most of my life. I've always had strange, very detailed dreams, of different lives and different times, so I accepted all of this long before I was old enough to think it was impossible." He gave a harsh laugh as he too sought fortitude in caffeine. "Knowing about you, waiting for you, ruined me for other women. I won't lie and say I've been as chaste as a monk, but I've never had even a teenage crush." He looked up at her, and his gaze was stark. "How could a giggling teen girl compete?" he whispered. "When I had the other memories, when I knew what it was to be a man, and make love to you?"

She hadn't had those memories until recently, but still she had gone through life romantically unscathed, the deepest part of her unable to respond to the men who had been interested in her. From the first, though, she hadn't been able to maintain any buffer against Richard. Both mentally and physically, she was painfully aware of him. He had grown up with this awareness, and it couldn't have been easy. It was difficult to picture, but at one time he had been a child, and in effect he had been robbed of a normal childhood and adolescence, of a normal *life*.

"As to how I found you," he continued, "the dreams led me here. The details I saw helped me narrow down the location. The dreams were getting stronger, and I knew you couldn't be far away. As soon as I saw this place, I knew this was it. So I rented the neighboring house, and waited."

"Where is your home?" she asked curiously.

He gave her an odd little smile. "I've lived in North Carolina for some time now."

She had the definite feeling that he wasn't telling her the entire truth. She sat back and studied him, considering her next question before voicing it. "What do you do for a living?"

He laughed, and there was a tone at once rueful and joyous in the sound, as if he'd expected her to pin him down. "God, some things never change. I'm in the military, what else?"

Of course. He was a warrior born, in whatever

73

lifetime. Snippets of information, gleaned from news broadcasts, slipped into place. With her inborn knowledge of him directing her, she hazarded a guess. "Fort Bragg?"

He nodded.

Special Forces, then. She wouldn't have known where they were based, if it hadn't been for all the news coverage during the Gulf War. A sudden terror seized her. Had he been in that conflict? What if he had been killed, and she had never known about him—

Then she wouldn't now have to fear for her own life.

Somehow that didn't mitigate the fear she felt for him. She had always been afraid for him. He lived with danger, and shrugged at it, but she had never been able to do that.

"How did you get leave?"

"I had a lot of time due. I don't have to go back for another month, unless something unexpected happens." But there was a strained expression deep in his eyes, a resignation that she couldn't quite read.

He reached across the table and took her hand. His long, callused fingers wrapped around her slimmer, smaller ones, folding them in warmth. "What about you? Where do you live, what do you do?"

The safest thing would be not to tell him, but she doubted there was any point in it. After all, he had her name, and he probably had her license plate number. If he wanted to, he would be able to find her. "I live in White Plains. I grew up there; all of my family lives there." She found herself rattling on, suddenly anxious to fill him in on the details of her life. "My parents are still alive, and I have two brothers, one older and one younger. Do you have any brothers or sisters?"

He shook his head, smiling at her. "I have a couple of aunts and uncles, and some cousins scattered around the country, but no one close."

He had always been a loner, allowing no one to get close to him—except for her. In that respect, he had been as helpless as she.

"I paint houses," she said, still driven by the compulsion to fill all the gaps in their knowledge of each other. "The actual houses, not pictures of them. And I do murals." She felt herself tense, wanting him to approve, rather than express the incredulity some people did.

His fingers tightened on hers, then relaxed. "That makes sense. You've always loved making our surroundings as beautiful and comfortable as possible, whether it was a fur on the floor of the tent or wildflowers in a metal cup."

Until he spoke, she'd had no memory of those things, but suddenly she saw the pelts she had used to make their pallet on the tent floor, and the way the wildflowers, which she had arranged in a metal cup, had nodded their heads in the rush of cold air every time the flap was opened.

"Do you remember everything?" she whispered.

"Every detail? No. I can't remember every detail that's happened in this life, either; no one does. But the important things, yes."

"How many times have we . . ." Her voice trailed off as she was struck once again by the impossibility of it.

"Made love?" he suggested, though he knew darn well that wasn't what she had been about to say. Still, his eyes took on a heated, sleepy expression. "Times without number. I've never been able to get enough of you."

Her body jolted with responding desire

Sternly she controlled it. It would mean her life if she gave in to the aching need to become involved with him again. "Lived," she corrected.

She sensed his reluctance to tell her, but he had sworn he would answer all her questions, and his word was his bond. "Twelve," he said, tightening his hand on hers again. "This is our twelfth time."

She nearly jumped out of her chair. Twelve! The number echoed in her head. She had remembered only half of those times, and those memories were partial. Overwhelmed, she tried to pull away from him. She couldn't keep her sanity under such an overload.

Somehow she found herself drawn around the table, and settled on his lap. She accepted the familiarity of the position, knowing that he had held her this way many times. His thighs were hard under her bottom, his chest a solid bulwark to shield her, his arms supporting bands of living steel. It didn't make sense that she should feel so safe and protected in the embrace of a man who was so much of a danger to her, but the contact with his body was infinitely comforting.

He was saying something reassuring, but Thea couldn't concentrate on the words. She tilted her head back against his shoulder, dizzy with the tumult of warring emotions. He looked down at her and caught his breath, falling silent as his gaze settled on her mouth.

She knew she should turn away, but she didn't, couldn't. Instead her arm slipped up around his neck, holding tightly to him as he bent his head and covered her mouth with his.

7

The taste of him was like coming home, their mouths fitting together without any awkwardness or uncertainty. A growl of hunger rumbled in his throat, and his entire body tensed as he took her mouth with his tongue. With the ease of long familiarity he thrust his hand under her T-shirt and closed it over her breast, working his fingers beneath the lace of the bra cup so his hand was on her bare skin, her nipple beading against his palm. Thea shuddered under his touch, a paroxysm of mingled desire and relief, as if she had been holding herself tightly against the pain of his absence and could only now relax. There had never been another man for her, she thought dimly as she sank under the pleasure of his kiss, and never would be. Though they seemed to be caught in a hellish death-dance, she could no more stop loving him than she could stop her own heartbeat.

His response to her was as deep and uncontrollable as hers was to him. She felt it in the quivering tension of his body, the raggedness of his breathing, the desperate need so plain in his touch. Why then, in all of their lives together, had he destroyed her? Tears seeped from beneath her lashes as she clung to him. Was it *because* of the force of his need? Had he been unable to bear being so much at the mercy of someone else, found his vulnerability to be intolerable, and in a sudden fury lashed out to end that need? No; she rejected that scenario, because one of her clearest memories was of the calmness in his aquamarine eyes as he'd forced her deeper into the water, holding her down until there was no more oxygen in her lungs and her vision clouded over.

A teardrop ran into the corner of her mouth, and he tasted the saltiness. He groaned, and his lips left her mouth to slide over her cheek, sipping up the moisture. He didn't ask why she was crying, didn't become anxious or uneasy. Instead he simply held her closer, silently comforting her with his presence. He had never been discomfited by her tears, Thea remembered, past scenes sliding through her memory like silken scarves, wispy but detectable. Not that she had ever been a weepy kind of person anyway; and when she *had* cried, more often than not he had been the cause of her tears. His response then had always been exactly what it was now: he'd held her, let her cry it out, and seldom veered from his set course, no matter how upset he'd made her.

"You've never compromised worth a damn," Thea muttered, turning her face into his shoulder to use his shirt as a handkerchief.

He effortlessly followed her chain of thought. He sighed as his fingers gently kneaded her breast, savoring the silkiness of her skin, the pebbling of her nipple. "We were always on opposite sides. I couldn't betray my country, my friends."

"But you expected *me* to," she said bitterly.

"No, never. Your memories are still cloudy and incomplete, aren't they? Sweetheart, you made some difficult decisions, but they were based on your own sense of justice, not because I coerced you."

"So you say." She grasped his wrist and shoved his hand out from under her shirt. "Because my memory is cloudy, I can't argue that point, can I?"

"You could try trusting me." The statement was quiet, his gaze intent.

"You keep saying that." She stirred restlessly on his lap. "Under the circumstances, that seems to be asking a bit much, don't you think? Or am I safe with you, as long as we stay away from water?"

His mouth took on a bitter curve. "Trust has always been our problem." Lifting his hand, the one that had so recently cupped her breast, he toyed with one of her wayward curls. "On my part, too, I admit. I was never certain you wouldn't change your mind and betray me, instead."

"Instead of my father, you mean." Suddenly furious, she tried to struggle out of his lap. He simply tightened his arms, holding her in place as he had many times before.

"Your temper never changes," he observed, delight breaking through the grimness of his mood.

"I don't have a temper," Thea snapped, knowing full well her brothers would instantly disagree with that statement. She didn't have a hair-trigger temper, but she didn't back down from much, either.

"Of course you don't," he crooned, cuddling her closer, and the absolute love in his voice nearly broke her heart. How could he feel so intensely about her and still do what he did? And how could she still love him so much in return?

He held her in silence for a while, his heartbeat thudding against the side of her breast. The sensation was one she had felt many times before, lying cuddled on his left arm so his right arm, the one that wielded his sword, was unencumbered.

She wanted this, she realized. She wanted *him*, for a lifetime. For forever. In all their previous lifetimes, their time together had been numbered in months or even mere weeks, their loving so painfully intense she had sometimes panicked at the sheer force of what she was feeling. They had never been able to grow old together, to love each other without desperation or fear. Now she had a vital decision to make: should she run, and protect her life . . . or stay, and fight for their life together? The common sense that had ruled her life, at least until the dreams had disrupted everything, said to run. Her heart told her to hold to him as tightly as she could. Maybe, just maybe, if she was very cautious, she could win this time. She would have to be extremely wary of situations involving water. With the perfection of hindsight, she knew now that going to see the turtles with him had been fool-hardy; she was lucky nothing bad had happened. Probably it simply wasn't time, yet, for whatever had happened in the past to happen again.

Things were different this time, she realized. Their circumstances were different. A thrill went through her as she realized that this time *could* be different. "We aren't on opposing sides, this time," she whispered. "My father is a wonderful, perfectly ordinary family man, without an army to his name."

Richard chuckled, but quickly sobered. When Thea looked up, she saw the grimness in his eyes. "We have to get it right," he said quietly. "This is our twelfth time. I don't think we'll have another chance."

Thea drew back from him a little. "It would help if I understood why you did . . . what you did.

I've never known. *Tell* me, Richard. That way I can guard against—"

He shook his head. "I can't. It all comes down to trust. That's the key to it all. I have to trust you. You have to trust me . . . *even in the face of overwhelming evidence to the contrary.*"

"That's asking a lot," she pointed out in a dry tone. "Do you have to trust me to the same extent?"

"I already have." One corner of his mouth twitched in a wry smile. "The last time. That's probably why our circumstances have changed."

"What happened?"

"I can't tell you that, either. That would be changing the order of things. You either remember or you don't. We either get it right this time, or we lose forever."

She didn't like the choices. She wanted to scream at him, vent her fury at the mercilessness of fate, but knew it wouldn't do any good. She could only fight her own battle, knowing that it would mean her life if she failed. Maybe that was the point of it all, that each person was ultimately responsible for his or her own life. If so, she didn't much care for the lesson.

He began kissing her again, tilting her head up

and drinking deeply from her mouth. Thea could have reveled in his kisses for hours, but all too soon he was drawing back, his breath ragged and desire darkening his eyes. "Lie down with me," he whispered. "It's been so long. I need you, Thea."

He did. His erection was iron-hard against her bottom. Still, for all the intimacy of their past lives, in *this* life she had only just met him, and she was reluctant to let things go so far, so fast. He saw her refusal in her expression before she could speak, and muttered a curse under his breath.

"You do this every time," he said in raw frustration. "You drive me crazy. Either you make me wait when I'm dying to have you, or you tease me into making love to you when I know damn well I shouldn't."

"Is that so?" Thea slipped off his lap and gave him a sultry glance over her shoulder. She had never given anyone a sultry glance before, and was mildly surprised at herself for even knowing how, but the gesture had come naturally. Perhaps, in the past, she had been a bit of a temptress. She liked the idea. It felt right. Richard's personality was so strong that she needed *something* to help keep him in line.

He glowered at her, and his hands clenched into fists. If they had been further along in their relationship, she thought, he wouldn't have taken no for an answer, at least not yet. First he would have made a damn good effort at seducing her— an effort that had usually succeeded. Whatever his name, and whatever the time, Richard had always been a devastatingly sensual lover. But he too felt the constraints of newness, knew that she was still too skittish for what he wanted.

Stiffly he got to his feet, wincing in discomfort. "In that case, we should get out of here, maybe drive into town for lunch. Or breakfast," he amended, glancing at his wristwatch.

Thea smiled, both amused and touched by his thoughtfulness. Being in public with him did seem a lot safer than staying here. "Just like a date," she said, and laughed. "We've never done that before."

IT WAS A DELIGHTFUL DAY, full of the joy of rediscovery. After eating breakfast at the lone café in the small nearby town, they drove the back roads, stopping occasionally to get out and explore on foot. Richard carefully avoided all streams and

87

ponds, so Thea was relaxed, and could devote herself to once again learning to know this man she had always loved. So many things he did triggered memories, some of them delicious and some disturbing. To say their past lives together had been tumultuous would have been to understate the matter. She was shocked to remember the time she had used a knife to defend herself from him, an encounter that had ended in bloodletting: his. And in lovemaking.

But with each new memory, she felt more complete, as the missing parts slipped into place. She felt as if she had been only one-dimensional for the twenty-nine years of her life, and only now was becoming a full, real person.

And there were new things to discover about him. He hadn't been freeze-dried; he was a modern man, with memories and experiences that didn't include her. Occasionally he used an archaic term or phrasing that amused her, until she caught herself doing the same thing.

"I wonder why we remember, this time," she mused as they strolled along a deserted lane, with the trees growing so thickly overhead that they formed a cool, dim tunnel. They had left his Jeep a hundred yards back, pulled to the side so it wouldn't block the nonexistent traffic. "We never did before."

"Maybe because this is the *last* time." He held her hand in his. She wanted to just stare at him, to absorb the details of his erect, military bearing, the arrogant angle of his dark head, the stubborn jut of his jaw. Panic filled her at the thought of this being the end, of losing him forever if she didn't manage to outwit fate.

She tightened her fingers on his. That was what she had to do: fight fate. If she won, she'd have a life with this man she had loved for two millennia. If she lost, she would die. It was that simple.

8

The next morning, Thea lay motionless in the predawn hour, her breath sighing in and out in the deep, easy rhythm of sleep. The dream began to unfold, as long-ago scenes played out in her unconsciousness.

The lake was silent and eerily beautiful in the dawn. She stood on the dock and watched the golden sun rise from behind the tall, dark trees, watched the lake turn from black to deep rose as it reflected the glow of the sky. She loved the lake in all its moods, but sunrise was her favorite. She waited, and was rewarded by the haunting cry of a loon as the lake awoke and greeted the day.

Her child moved within her, a gentle fluttering as

tiny limbs stretched. She smiled, and her hand slipped down to rest atop the delicate movement. She savored the feel of that precious life. Her child—and his. For five months now she had harbored it within her, delighting in each passing day as her body changed more and more. The slight swell of her belly was only now becoming noticeable. She had been in seclusion here at the lake, but soon her condition would be impossible to hide. She would face that problem, and her father's rage, when it became necessary, but she wouldn't let anything harm this child.

She still woke up aching for the presence of her lover, weeping for him, for what might have been had he been anyone else, had she been anyone else. Damn men, and damn their wars. She would have chosen him, had he given her the chance, but he hadn't. Instead he had simply ridden out of her life, not trusting her to love him enough. He didn't know about the new life he had left inside her.

The dock suddenly vibrated beneath her as booted feet thudded on the boards. Startled, she turned, and then stood motionless with shock, wondering if she was dreaming or if her longing had somehow conjured him out of the dawn. Faint wisps of mist swirled around him as he strode toward her. Her heart squeezed painfully. Even if he wasn't real, she thanked God for this chance to see him so clearly again—his thick dark hair, his vibrant, sea-colored eyes, the muscular perfection of his body.

Five feet from her he stopped, as suddenly as if he had hit a wall. His incredulous gaze swept down her body, so clearly outlined in the thin nightgown that was all she wore, with the sun shining behind her. He saw her hand resting protectively on the swell of her belly, in the instinctive touch of a pregnant woman.

He was real. Dear God, he was real. He had come back to her. She saw his shock mirrored in his eyes as he confronted the reality of impending fatherhood. He stared at her belly for a long, silent moment before dragging his gaze back up to hers. "Why didn't you tell me?" he asked hoarsely.

"I didn't know," she said. "Until after you'd gone."

He approached her, as cautiously as if confronting a wild animal, slowly reaching out his hand to rest it on her belly. She quivered at the heat and vitality of his touch, and nearly moaned aloud as the pain of months without him eased from her flesh. Couldn't he sense how much he had hurt her? Couldn't he tell that his absence had nearly killed her, that only the realization she was carrying his child had given her a reason to live?

And then she felt the quiver that ran through him,

too, as his hands closed on her body. Pure heat sizzled between them. She drew a deep, shaky breath of desire, her body softening and warming, growing moist for him in instinctive preparation.

"Let me see you," he groaned, already tugging her nightgown upward.

Somehow she found herself lying on the dock, her naked body bathed in the pearly morning light. The discarded nightgown protected her soft skin from the rough wood beneath her. The water lapped softly around her, beneath her, yet not touching her. She felt as if she were floating, anchored only by those strong hands. She closed her eyes, giving him privacy to acquaint himself with all the changes in her body, the changes she knew so intimately. His rough hands slipped over her as lightly as silk, touching her darkened, swollen nipples, cupping the fuller weight of her breasts in his palms. Then they moved down to her belly, framing the small, taut mound of his child.

She didn't open her eyes, even when he parted her legs, raising her knees and spreading them wide so he could look at her. She caught her breath at the cool air washing over her most intimate flesh, and the longing for him intensified. Couldn't he sense how much she needed him, couldn't he feel the vibrancy of her body under his hands? Of course he could. She had never been able to disguise her desire for him, even when she had desperately tried. She heard the rhythm of his breathing become ragged, and glowed with the knowledge of his desire.

"You're so lovely, it hurts to look at you," he whispered. She felt one long, callused finger explore the delicacies between her legs, stroking and rubbing before sliding gently inward. Her senses spun with the shock of that small invasion; her back arched off the dock, and he soothed her with a deep murmur. And then she felt him moving closer, positioning himself between her legs, adjusting his clothing, and she lay there in an agony of anticipation waiting for the moment when they would be together again, one again, whole again. He filled her so smoothly that he might have been part of her, and they both gasped at the perfection of it. Then the time for rational thought was past, and they could only move together, cling together, his strength complemented by her delicacy, male and female, forever mated.

Thea moaned in her sleep as her dream lover brought her to ecstasy, and then became still again as the dream altered, continued.

The water closed over her head, a froth of white marking the surface where she had gone under. The shock of it, after the ecstasy she had just known with him, paralyzed her for long, precious moments. Then she thought of the baby she carried, and silently screamed her fury that it should be endangered. She began struggling wildly against the inexorable grip that was tugging her downward, away from air, away from life. She couldn't let anything happen to this baby, no matter what its father had done. Despite everything, she loved him, loved his child.

But she couldn't kick free of the bond that dragged her down. Her nightgown kept twisting around her legs, instead of floating upward. Her lungs heaved in agony, trying to draw in air. She fought the impulse, knowing that she would inhale only death. Fight. She had to fight for her baby.

Powerful hands were on her shoulders, pushing her deeper into the water. Despairing, her vision failing, she stared through the greenish water into the cool, remote eyes of the man she loved so much she would willingly have followed him anywhere. He was forcing her down, down, away from the life-giving air.

"Why?" she moaned, the word soundless. The deadly water filled her mouth, her nostrils, rushed down her throat. She couldn't hold on much longer. Only the baby gave her the strength to continue fighting, as she struggled against those strong hands, trying to push him away. Her baby . . . she had to save her baby. But the

darkness was increasing, clouding over her eyes, and she knew that she had lost. Her last thought in this life was a faint, internal cry of despair: "Why?"

Helpless sobs shook Thea's body as she woke. She curled on her side, overwhelmed by grief, grief for her unborn child, grief for the man she had loved so much that not even her destruction at his hands had been able to kill her feelings for him. *It didn't make sense.* He had made love to her, and then he had drowned her. How could a man feel his own child kicking in its mother's belly, and then deliberately snuff out that helpless life? Regardless of how he felt about her, how could he have killed his baby?

The pain was shattering. She heard the soft, keening sound of her sobs as she huddled there, unable to move, unable to think.

Then she heard the Jeep, sliding to a hard stop in the driveway, its tires slinging gravel. She froze, terror running like ice water through her veins. He was here. She should have remembered that he had the same dreams she did; he knew that *she* knew about those last nightmarish moments beneath the water. She couldn't begin to think what he was trying to accomplish by repeating her death over and over through the ages, but suddenly she had no doubt that, if she remained there, she would shortly suffer the same fate again. After that last dream, there was no way he could sweet-talk her out of her fear the way he had done before.

She jumped out of bed, not taking the time to grab her clothes. Her bare feet were silent as she raced from the bedroom, across the living room, and into the kitchen. She reached the back door just as his big fist thudded against the front one. "Thea." His deep voice was forceful, but restrained, as if he were trying to convince her she wasn't in any danger.

The deep shadows of early dawn still shrouded the rooms, the graying light too weak to penetrate beyond the windows. Like a small animal trying to escape notice by a predator, Thea held herself very still, her head cocked as she listened for the slightest sound of his movements.

Could she slip out the back door without making any betraying noise? Or was he even now moving silently around the house in order to try this very door? The thought of opening the door and coming face-to-face with him made her blood run even colder than it already was.

"Thea, listen to me."

He was still on the front porch. Thea fumbled for the chain, praying that her shaking hands wouldn't betray her. She found the slot and slowly, agonizingly, slid the chain free, holding the links in her hand so they wouldn't clink. Then she reached for the lock.

"It isn't what you think, sweetheart. Don't be afraid of me, please. Trust me."

Trust him! She almost laughed aloud, the hysterical bubble moving upward despite her best efforts. She finally choked the sound back. He'd said that so often that the two words had become a litany. Time and again she had trusted him—with her heart, her body, the life of her child—and each time he had turned on her.

She found the lock, silently turned it.

"Thea, I know you're awake. I know you can hear me."

She opened the door by increments, holding her breath against any squeaks that would alert him. An inch of space showed gray light coming through the slot. Dawn was coming closer by the second, bringing with it the bright light that would make it impossible for her to hide from him. She didn't have her car keys, she realized, and the knowledge almost froze her in place. But she didn't dare go back for them; she would have to escape on foot. That might be best anyway. If she were in the car, he would easily be able to follow her. She felt far more vulnerable on foot, but hiding would be much easier.

Finally the door was open enough that she could slip through. She held her breath as she left the precarious safety of the house. She wanted to cower behind its walls, but knew that he would soon break a window and get in, or kick down the door. He was a warrior, a killer. He could get in. She wasn't safe there.

The back stoop wasn't enclosed, just a couple of steps with an awning overhead to keep out the rain. There was a screen door there, too. Cautiously she unlatched it, and began the torturous process of easing it open, nerves drawing tighter and tighter. Fiercely she concentrated, staring at the spring coil, willing it to silence. There was a tiny creak, one that couldn't have been audible more than a few feet away, but sweat dampened her body. An inch, two inches, six. The opening grew wider. Eight inches. Nine. She began to slip through.

Richard came around the side of the house. He saw her and sprang forward, like a great hunting beast.

Thea cried out and jumped backward, slamming the kitchen door and fumbling with the lock. Too late! He would come through that door, lock or not. She sensed his determination and left the lock undone, choosing instead an extra second of time as she sprinted for the front door.

The back door slammed open just as she reached the front. It was still locked. Her chest heaved with panic, her breath catching just behind her breastbone and going no deeper. Her shaking, jerking fingers tried to manipulate the chain, the lock.

"Thea!" his voice boomed, reverberating with fury.

Sobbing, she jerked the door open and darted out onto the porch, shoving the outside screen door open, too, launching herself through it, stumbling, falling to her knees in the tall, wet grass.

He burst through the front door. She scrambled to her feet, pulled the hem of her nightgown to her knees, and ran for the road.

"Damn it, listen to me!" he shouted, sprinting to cut her off. She swerved as he lunged in front of her, but he managed once again to get between her and the road.

Despair clouded her vision; sobs choked her. She was cornered. He was going to kill her, and once again she was helpless to protect herself.

She let her nightgown drop, the folds covering her feet, as she stared at him with tear-blurred eyes. The gray light was stronger now; she could see the fierceness of his eyes, the set of his jaw, the sheen of perspiration on his skin. He wore only a pair of jeans. No shirt, no shoes. His powerful chest rose and fell with his breathing, but he wasn't winded at all, while she was exhausted. She had no chance against him.

Slowly she began to back away from him, the pain inside her unfurling until it was all she could do to breathe, for her heart to keep beating. "How could you?" she sobbed, choking on the words. "Our baby . . . *How could you?*"

"Thea, listen to me." He spread his hands in an open gesture meant to reassure her, but she knew too much about him to be fooled. He didn't need a weapon; he could kill with his bare hands. "Calm down, sweetheart. I know you're upset, but come inside with me and we'll talk."

Angrily she dashed the tears from her cheeks. "Talk! What good would that do?" she shrieked. "Do you deny that it happened? You didn't just kill me, you killed our child, too!" Still she backed away, the pain too intense to let her remain even that close to him. She felt as if she were being torn apart inside, the grief so raw and unmanageable that she felt as if she would welcome death now, to escape this awful pain.

He looked beyond her, and his expression shifted, changed. A curious blankness settled in his eyes. His entire body tensed as he seemed to gather himself, as if he were about to spring. "You're getting too close to the water," he said in a flat, emotionless voice. "Come away from the bank."

Thea risked a quick glance over her shoulder, and saw that she was on the edge of the bank, the cool, deadly lake lapping close to her bare feet. Her tears blurred the image, but it was there, silently waiting to claim her.

The unreasoning fear of the lake gnawed at her, but was as nothing when measured against the unrelenting grief for her child. She changed the angle of her retreat, moving toward the dock. Richard kept pace with her, not advancing any closer, but not leaving her any avenue of escape, either. The inevitability of it all washed over her. She had thought she could outwit fate, but her efforts had been useless from the very beginning.

Her bare feet touched wood, and she retreated onto the dock. Richard halted, his aquamarine gaze fastened on her. "Don't go any farther," he said sharply. "The dock isn't safe. Some of the boards are rotten and loose. Come off the dock, baby. Come to me. I swear I won't hurt you."

Baby. Shards of pain splintered her insides, and she moaned aloud, her hand going to her belly as if her child still rested there. Desperately she backed away from him, shaking her head.

He set one foot on the dock. "I can't bring that child back," he said hoarsely. "But I'll give you another one. We'll have as many children as you want. Don't leave me this time, Thea. For God's sake, let's get off this dock."

"Why?" Tears were still blurring her vision, running down her cheeks, a bottomless well of grief. "Why put it off? Why not get it over with now?" She moved back still more, feeling the boards creak and give beneath her bare feet. The water was quite deep at the end of the dock; it had been perfect for three boisterous kids to dive and frolic in, without fear of hitting their heads on the bottom. If she was destined to die here, then so be it. Water. It was always water. She had always loved it, and it had always claimed her in the end.

Richard slowly stepped forward, never taking his eyes off her, his hand outstretched. "Please. Just take my hand, darling. Don't move back any more. It isn't safe."

"Stay away from me!" she shrieked.

"I can't." His lips barely moved. "I never could." He took another step. "Thea—"

Hastily, she stepped back. The board gave beneath her weight, then began to crack. She felt one side collapse beneath her, pitching her sideways into the water. She had only a blurred, confused image of Richard leaping forward, his face twisting with helpless rage, before the water closed over her head.

It was cool, murky. She went down, pulled by some unseen hand. The darkness of the dock pilings drifted in front of her as she went deeper, deeper. After all the terror and pain, it was almost a relief for it to end, and for a long moment she simply gave in to the inevitable. Then instinct took over, as irresistible as it was futile, and she began fighting, trying to kick her way to the surface. But her nightgown was twisted around her legs, pulling tighter and tighter the more she struggled, and she realized that she had caught it in the broken boards. The boards were pulling her down, and with her legs bound she couldn't generate enough energy to counteract their drag.

If she could have laughed, she would have. This time, Richard wouldn't have to do anything. She had managed to do the deed herself. Still, she didn't stop fighting, trying to swim against the pull of the boards.

The surface roiled with his dive, as he cut through the water just to her left. Visibility was poor, but she could see the gleam of his skin, the darkness of his hair. He spotted her immediately, the white of her nightgown giving away her position, and he twisted his body in her direction.

Anger speared through her. He just had to see it through; he couldn't let the lake do its work without his aid. Probably he wanted to make certain she didn't fight her way free.

She put up her hands to ward him off, redoubling her efforts to reach the surface. She was using up all her oxygen in her struggles, and her lungs were burning, heaving with the need to inhale. Richard caught her flailing hands and began pushing her down, down, farther away from the light, from life.

Thea saw his eyes, calm and remote, every atom of his being concentrated on what he was doing. She had little time left, so very little. Pain swirled inside her, and anger at the fate that was hers, despite her best efforts. Desperately she tried to jerk free of him, using the last of her strength for one final effort. . . .

Despite everything, she had always loved him so much, beyond reason, even beyond death.

That was an even deeper pain: the knowledge that she was leaving him forever. Their gazes met through the veil of murky water, his face so close to hers that she could have kissed him, and through the growing darkness she saw her anguish mirrored in his eyes. *Trust me*, he'd said repeatedly. *Trust me . . . even in the face of overwhelming evidence to the contrary. Trust me. . . .*

Trust him.

Realization spread through Thea like a sunburst. Trust. She had never been able to trust him, or in

his love for her. They had been like two wary animals, longing to be together, but not daring to let
themselves be vulnerable to the other. They hadn't
trusted. And they had paid the price.

Trust him.

She stopped struggling, letting herself go limp,
letting him do what he would. She had no more
strength anyway. Their gazes still held, and with
her eyes she gave herself to him, her love shining
through. Ever if it was too late, she wanted him to
know that in the end, no matter what, she loved
him.

She saw his pupils flare, felt his renewed effort
as he pushed her down, all the way to the bottom.
Then, without the weight of the boards dragging
at her, he was able to get enough slack in the fabric of her nightgown to work it free of the entan-
gling wood. The last bubble of air escaped her lips
as he wrapped his arm around her waist and used
his powerful legs to propel them upward, to the
surface and wonderful oxygen, to life.

"GOD, PLEASE, PLEASE, oh God, please." She
heard his desperate, muttered prayer as he
dragged her out of the water, but she couldn't

respond, couldn't move, as she flopped like a rag
doll in his arms. Her lungs weren't quite working;
she couldn't drag in the deep, convulsive breaths
that she needed.

Richard dropped her on the grass and began
pounding her on the back. Her lungs jerked, then
heaved, and she coughed up a quantity of lake
water. He continued to beat her on the back, until
she thought he would break her ribs.

"I'm . . . all . . . right," she managed to gasp,
trying to evade that thumping fist. She coughed
some more, gagging.

He collapsed beside her in his own paroxysm of
coughing, his muscular chest heaving as he fought
for air.

Thea struggled onto her side, reaching for him,
needing to touch him. They lay in the grass, shivering and coughing, as the first warming rays of
the sun crept across the lake to touch them.
Convulsively he clasped her to him, tears running
down his cheeks, muttering incoherently as he
pressed desperate kisses to her face, her throat.
His big body was taut, shaking with a tension that
wouldn't relent. He rolled her beneath him, jerking the sodden folds of her nightgown to her

waist. Thea felt his desperate, furious need, and lay still as he fought with the wet, stubborn fabric of his jeans, finally getting them open and peeling them down. He pushed her legs open and stabbed into her, big and hot and so hard that she cried out even as she held him as tightly as she could.

He rode her hard and fast, needing this affirmation that they both still lived, needing this link with her. Thea's response soared out of control and she climaxed almost immediately, crying out with the joy of having him there with her as she clung to him with arms and legs. He bucked wildly, shuddered, and she felt the warm flood of his orgasm within her, then he fell onto the grass beside her.

He lay there holding her for a long time, her head cradled on his shoulder, neither of them able to stop touching the other. He smoothed back her unruly tumble of curls; she stroked his chest, his arms. He kissed her temple; she nuzzled his jaw. He squeezed and stroked her breasts; her hands kept wandering down to his naked loins. She imagined they made quite a picture of debauchery, lying there on the ground with her nightgown hiked to her waist and his jeans down around his knees, but the sun was warm and she was drowsy, her body replete with satisfaction, and she didn't much care.

Eventually he moved, kicking his legs free of the damp jeans. She smiled as he stretched out, blissfully naked. He had never been blessed with an overabundance of modesty. But then, it was almost a crime to cover up a body like his. She sighed with her own bliss, thinking of the naughty things she planned to do to him later, when they were sprawled out in that big bed. Some things required a mattress rather than grass. Though those pelts had been wonderful . . .

"All those times," she murmured, kissing his shoulder. "You were trying to save me."

His vivid eyes slitted open as he gathered her closer. "Of course," he said simply. "I couldn't live without you."

But you did. The comment died on her lips as she stared at him, reading his expression. His eyes were calm, and accepting. Emotion swelled in her chest until she could barely breathe, and tears glittered in her eyes. "Damn you," she said shakily. He *hadn't* lived. Each time, when he had failed to save her, he had remained there with her, choosing to share her death rather than live without her.

This had been his last chance as well as hers, and theirs. "Damn you," she said again, thumping him on the chest with her fist. "How could you do that? Why didn't you *live?*"

A slow smile touched his lips as he played with one of her curls. "Would you have?" he asked, and the smile grew when she scowled at him. No, she couldn't have left him in the water and gone on living. She would have remained with him.

"You little hellcat," he said contentedly, gathering her against his chest. "You've led me on quite a chase, but I've caught you now. We finally got it right."

Epilogue

Two days later Thea and Richard were sitting outside in the swing, which he had repaired, contentedly watching the lake. Her bare feet were in his lap and he was massaging them, saying he wanted to get in practice for when she was big with pregnancy and would need such services. Both of them were absurdly positive that their first lovemaking had been fertile, and her happiness was so intoxicating that she felt giddy.

Her fear of the water had disappeared as suddenly as it had formed. She hadn't been swimming yet, but that was more because of Richard's anxieties than her own. Whenever they walked, he still positioned himself between her and the water, and she wondered if he would ever relax his vigil.

Plans. They'd made a lot of plans for their life together. For one thing, she would be moving to North Carolina. Her warrior wasn't just "in" the Special Forces—he was a lieutenant colonel. Since he was only thirty-five, that meant he had a lot of time left to reach general, which was probably inevitable. Thea rather thought she would have to give up painting houses; it just wasn't the thing for a general's wife to do. The murals, though, were something else. . . .

For now, though, they were selfishly enjoying getting reacquainted with each other, hugging every moment of privacy to themselves. They had cleaned up the yard, and this morning they had started preparing the house for its new coat of paint. Most of the time, though, they had spent in bed.

She tilted her face up to the sun, and gently cupped her hand over her belly. It was there. She knew it was. She didn't need either drugstore or lab test to confirm what she felt in every cell of her body. Too tiny almost to be seen, as yet, but indubitably there.

Richard's hand covered hers, and she opened

her eyes to find him smiling at her. "Boy or girl?" he asked.

She hesitated. "What do you think?"

"I asked first."

"Let's say it together. You go first."

His mouth opened, then he stopped and narrowed his eyes at her. "Almost got you," she said smugly.

"Smart-ass. All right, it's a boy."

She twined her fingers with his, sighing with contentment. "I agree." A son. Richard's son. The baby who had died with her had been a daughter. She blinked back tears for that child, wondering if it was forever lost, or if it too had been given another chance.

"She'll have another chance," Richard whispered, gathering Thea close. "Maybe next time. We'll know."

Yes, they would. Each night, her memory became more complete as the dreams continued. Richard still shared them, and they would awaken to find their bodies locked together, ecstasy still pulsing through them. They were linked, body and soul, the past revealed to them as it was to only a few lucky people.

They heard the cars before they could see them, and Thea sat up, swinging her feet to the ground. Richard stood, automatically moving to place himself between her and whoever approached. Thea tugged on his belt and he looked around, a sheepish look crossing his face as he realized what he'd done.

"Old habits," he said, shrugging. *"Real old."*

Then the three cars came into view, and Thea watched in astonishment as her entire family drove up. It took her a moment to realize. "Today's my birthday!" she gasped. "I'd forgotten!"

"Birthday, huh?" He looped an arm over her shoulders. "How about that. That makes you . . . thirty, right? I have to tell you, this is the oldest you've ever been. But you're holding up good."

"Thank you so much." Grinning, she caught his hand and began tugging him forward. She'd see if he was so sassy after being overwhelmed by her family. Nieces and nephews were spilling out of open doors, running toward her, while adults unfolded themselves at a slower pace. Lee and Cynthia, Jason and June, and her mom and dad all approached a bit warily, as if afraid they had intruded on a romantic get-away.

"I didn't realize you'd brought company with you, dear," her mom said, looking Richard up and down with a mother's critical assessment.

Richard laughed, the sound low and easy. "She didn't," he said, holding out his hand to Thea's father. "My name is Richard Chance. I'm renting the house next door."

Her father grinned. "I'm Paul Marlow, Thea's father. This is my wife, Emily." Polite introductions were made all around, and Thea had to bite her lip to keep from laughing out loud. Though her father was perfectly relaxed, and both Cynthia and June were smiling happily at Richard, her mom and brothers were scowling suspiciously at the warrior in their midst.

Before anything embarrassing could be said, she slipped her arm through Richard's. "Lieutenant Colonel Richard Chance," she said mildly. "On leave from Fort Bragg, North Carolina. And, for the record, my future husband."

The words worked a sea change in her more pugnacious relatives. Amid a flurry of congratulations and squeals, plus tears from her mother, she heard her father say reflectively, "That's fast work. You've known each other, what, four or five days?"

"No," Richard said with perfect aplomb. "We've known each other off and on for years, but the timing wasn't right. Everything worked out this time, though. I guess it was just meant to be."

BLUE MOON

1

One full moon a month was bad enough, Sheriff Jackson Brody thought sourly; two should be outlawed. Nature's rule of survival of the fittest had been all but negated by humans, with advances in modern medicine and the generally held view that all life was worth saving, with the result that there were a lot of very weird, and/or stupid people out there, and they all seemed to surface during a full moon.

He was not in a good mood after working a car accident on a county road. As sheriff, his duties were not supposed to include working wrecks, but damned if every full moon he didn't find himself doing exactly that. The county was small and poor, mostly rural, and couldn't afford the number of deputies he needed, so he was always juggling schedules anyway. Add the madness of a full moon to an understaffed department, and the problems multiplied.

The accident he had just worked made him so furious he had been stretching the limits of his willpower not to cuss at the participants. He couldn't call them *victims*, unless it was of their own stupidity. The only victim was the poor little boy who had been in the passenger seat of the car.

It all started when the driver of the first vehicle, a pickup truck, woke up and realized he had missed his turn by about a quarter of a mile. Instead of going on and finding a place to turn around, the idiot began backing up, going the wrong way down a narrow two-lane blacktop, around a blind curve. He was an accident waiting to happen, and he hadn't had to wait long. A woman came speeding around the curve, doing over sixty miles an hour on a road with a posted speed limit of thirty-five, and plowed into the rear of the pickup. She wasn't wearing a seatbelt.

Neither was the four-year-old sitting in the front seat. For that matter, neither was the driver of the pickup. It was nothing less than a miracle that all three had survived, though the little boy was severely injured and Jackson had seen enough accident victims to know his chances were no better than fifty-fifty, at best. The car had had airbags, at least, which had kept the two in the car from going through the windshield.

He had given the woman citations for reckless driving, not wearing a seatbelt, and not properly securing her child, and she began screaming at him. Had he ever tried to make a four-year-old sit down and wear a seatbelt? The blankety-blank things chafed her blankety-blank neck, and the state had no business telling people what they could do on their private property, which her car was, and the car had airbags anyway so there was no need for seatbelts, blah blah blah. There she was, with bulging eyes and unkempt hair, a living testament to the destructive power of recessive genes, throwing a hissy fit about getting traffic tickets while her screaming child was being carried away in an ambulance. Privately, Jackson thought people like her had no business having children in their care, but he made a heroic effort and kept the observation to himself.

Then the driver of the pickup, he of the bulging beer belly and breath that would fell a moose at fifty paces, added his opinion that he thought her driver's license should be taken away because this was all her fault for rear-ending him. When Jackson then gave *him* citations for reckless driving and driving in the wrong lane, he was enraged. This accident wasn't *his* fault, he bellowed, and damned if he was going to get stuck with higher insurance premiums because a stupid hick sheriff didn't know an accident was always the fault of the one doing the rear-ending. Any fool could look at where his truck was hit and tell who was at fault here.

Jackson didn't bother explaining the difference between the truck's hood being pointed in the right direction while the truck itself was going in reverse. He just wrote the tickets and in the accident report stated that both drivers were at fault, and seriously pondered whether or not he should lock these two up for the safety of the universe. Terminal stupidity wasn't on the books as a chargeable offense, but it should be, in his opinion.

But he restrained himself, and oversaw the

transportation of both furious drivers to the local hospital to be checked out, and the removal of the damaged vehicles. When he finally crawled back into his Jeep Cherokee it was pushing four o'clock, long past lunchtime. He was tired, hungry, and both angry and discouraged.

Generally he loved his work. It was a job where he could make a difference in people's lives, in society. Granted, it was usually scut work; he dealt with the worst of society, while having to maneuver on tippy-toes through a tangle of laws and regulations. But when everything worked and a drug dealer got sent away for a few years, or a murderer was put away forever, or a burglary gang was rounded up and an old lady on Social Security got her 19-inch television back, that made it all worthwhile.

He was a good sheriff, though he hated the political side of it, hated having to campaign for office. He was just thirty-five, young for the office, but the county was so poor it couldn't afford someone who was both good and with a lot of experience, because those people went where the pay was better. The citizens had taken a chance with him two years ago and he'd been doing his best at a job he loved. Not many people had that chance.

During full moons, however, he doubted his own sanity. He had to be a fool or an idiot, or both, to want a job that put him on the front lines during the periods of rampant weirdness. Cops and emergency-room personnel could all testify to the craziness that went on during a full moon.

A nurse at the local hospital, after reading a report that the tales about full moons were just myths, that the accident rate didn't really go up, kept a record for a year. Not only did the number of accidents go up, but that was when they got the really strange ones, like the guy who had his buddy nail his hands together so his wife wouldn't ask him to help with the housework on his day off. It was obvious to them: a man couldn't very well work with his hands nailed together, now could he? The scariest thing about it was that both of them had been sober.

So one full moon a month was all Jackson felt any human should be called upon to endure. A blue moon, the second full moon in a single month, fell under the heading of cruel and unusual punishment.

And because it was a blue moon, he wasn't surprised, when he radioed in that he was finished with the accident and heading for a bite to eat, that the dispatcher said, "You might want to hold off on the food, and check in on a secure line."

Jackson stifled a groan. A couple of clues told him he really didn't want to know what this one was. For one thing, though the radio traffic was usually businesslike, for the benefit of the good citizens who listened in on their scanners, the dispatcher had fallen into a more personal tone. And they didn't bother to check in on a secure line unless there was something going on they didn't want the listeners to know about, which meant it was either something sensitive like one of the town fathers acting up, or something personal. He hoped the issue was sensitive, because he sure as hell didn't feel like dealing with anything personal, like his mother running amuck at her regular Wednesday bingo game.

He picked up his digital cell phone and checked whether or not he had service in this part of the county; he did, though it wasn't the strongest signal. He flipped the cover open and dialed the dispatcher. "This is Brody. What's up?"

Jo Vaughn had been the dispatcher for ten years, and he couldn't think of anyone he would rather have on the job. Not only did she know just about every inhabitant of the small south Alabama county, something that had been a tremendous aid to him, but she also had an eerily accurate instinct for what was urgent and what wasn't. Sometimes the citizens involved might not agree, but Jackson always did.

"I've got a bad feeling," she announced. "Shirley Waters saw Thaniel Vargas hauling his flat-bottom down Old Boggy Road. There's nothing out that way except the Jones's place, and you know how Thaniel is."

Jackson took a moment to reflect. This was one of those times when growing up in west Texas instead of south Alabama was a definite handicap. He knew where Old Boggy Road was, but only because he had spent days looking at county maps and memorizing the roads. He had never personally been on Old Boggy, though. And he knew who Thaniel Vargas was; a slightly thick-headed troublemaker, the type found in every community. Thaniel was hot-tempered, a bit of a bully, and he liked his beer a little too much. He'd been in some trouble with the law, but nothing serious enough to rate more than a few fines and warnings.

Other than that, though, Jackson drew a blank. "Refresh me."

"Well, you know how superstitious he is."

His eyebrows lifted. He hadn't expected that. "No, I didn't know," he said dryly. "What does that have to do with him taking his boat down Old Boggy Road, and who are the Joneses?"

"Jones," Jo corrected. "There's just one now, since old man Jones died four—no, let's see, it was right after Beatrice Marbut's husband died in his girlfriend's trailer, so that would make it five years ago—"

Jackson closed his eyes and refrained from asking what difference it made how long ago old man Jones died. Hurrying a Southerner through a conversation was like trying to push a rope, though sometimes he couldn't stop himself from trying.

"—and Delilah's been out there alone ever since."

He took a wild stab at getting to the point of Jo's anxiety. "And Thaniel Vargas dislikes Mrs. Jones?"

"Miss. She's never been married."

The wild stab hadn't worked. "Then old man Jones was—"

"Her father."

"Okay." He tried again. "Why does Thaniel dislike Miss Jones?"

"Oh, I wouldn't say he *dislikes* her. It's more like he's scared to death of her."

He took a deep breath. "Because . . . ?"

"Because of the witch thing, of course."

That did it. Some things just weren't worth fighting. Jackson surrendered and let himself go with the flow. "Witch thing," he repeated. That was twice in one minute Jo had surprised him.

"You mean you never heard about that?" Jo sounded surprised.

"Not a word." He wished he wasn't hearing about it now.

"Well, folks think she's a witch. Not that I think so, mind, but I can see where some would be uneasy."

"Why is that?"

"Oh, she keeps to herself, hardly ever comes to town. And old man Jones was strange, didn't let anyone come around. Even the mail is delivered by boat, because there's no road going out to the Jones place. The only way to get there is to hike in, or by the river." Background established, she settled into her explanation. "Now, if Thaniel was going fishing, the best fishing is downriver, not up. There's no reason he'd be launching a boat from the Old Boggy ramp unless he was going upriver, and there's nothing up there but the Jones place. He wouldn't have the nerve unless he'd been drinking, because he's so afraid of Delilah, so I think you need to go out there and make sure he's not up to no good."

Jackson wondered how many sheriffs were bossed around by their dispatchers. He wondered just what the hell he was supposed to do, since Jo had just told him the only way to get to the Jones place was by boat. And he wondered, not for the first time, whether or not he was going to survive this damn blue moon.

Well, until it killed him, he had a job to do. He assessed the situation and began solving the most immediate problems. "Call Frank at the Rescue Squad and tell him to meet me at the launch ramp on Old Boggy—"

"You don't want one of the Rescue Squad boats," Jo interrupted. "They're too slow, and the guys are all helping with the cleanup at the tractor-trailer wreck out on the big highway, anyway. I called Charlotte Watkins. Her husband's a bass fisherman—you know Jerry Watkins, don't you?"

"I've met both of them," Jackson said.

"He's got one of those real fast boats. He's gone to Chattanooga on business, but Charlotte was going to hook up the boat and take it to the ramp. She should be there by the time you get there."

"Okay," he said, "I'm on my way." He pinched the top of his nose, between his eyebrows, feeling a headache beginning to form. He wished he could ignore Jo's intuition, but it was too accurate for him to doubt her. "Send some backup as soon as someone comes available. And how in hell do I find the Jones place?"

"Just go upriver, you can't miss it. It's about five miles up. The house is hard to see, it kind of blends in, but it's dead ahead and you'll think you're going to run right into it, but then the river curves real sharp to the right and gets too shallow to go much farther. Oh, and be careful of the snags. Stay in the middle of the river." She paused. "You *do* know how to drive a boat, don't you?"

"I'll figure it out," he said, and flipped the phone cover down to end the call. Let her stew for a while, wondering if she had made a bad mistake sending the sheriff out alone into a possibly dangerous situation, on a river he didn't know and in a piece of powerful equipment he didn't know how to operate. He'd driven a boat for the first time at the age of eleven, but Jo didn't know that, and it would do her good to realize she wasn't omnipotent.

He didn't use his lights or siren, but he did jam his boot down on the accelerator and keep it there. By his estimation he was at least fifteen minutes from Old Boggy Road, and he had no idea how far down the road the launch ramp was. In a powerful boat he could easily go sixty miles an hour, putting him at the Jones place in five minutes or less, once he was on the water. That meant it would take him at least twenty minutes to get there, probably longer. If Thaniel Vargas was up to no good, Jackson was afraid he would have plenty of time to accomplish it.

He felt a surge of adrenaline, the surge every law enforcement officer felt when going into a potentially dangerous situation. He hoped he wouldn't find anything out of the ordinary, though. He hoped like hell he wouldn't, because if he did, that would mean Miss Jones—had Jo actually said her name was *Delilah?*—was either hurt or dead.

Witch? Why hadn't he heard anything about this before? He'd lived here for three years, been sheriff for two, and in that time he thought he'd learned about all the county's unusual citizens. There hadn't been a peep about Delilah Jones, though, not from his deputies, not from the mayor or her secretary, who was the most gossipy person Jackson had ever met, not from the bar crowd or the women he dated, not from the blue-haired bingo circuit, not even from Jo. He hadn't missed the fact that Jo seemed well-informed on how to get to the Jones house. How would she know that, unless she'd been there? And why would she go, considering everything she'd said about the Jones woman being reclusive and her father being strange?

If anyone was practicing witchcraft in his county, he should have known about it. It was all bullshit, in his opinion, but if anyone else took it seriously then there could be trouble. From the sound of things, that was exactly what was happening.

First there was the general blue-moon craziness, then the wreck between the two idiots, and now this. He was hungry, tired, and had a headache. He was beginning to get severely pissed.

2

Jackson reached Old Boggy Road in record time and churned down it, his tires digging in and throwing sand. The river was to his right, so he kept an eye in that direction, looking for the launch ramp. The old road narrowed and became one rutted lane, with massive live oaks on each side intertwining their branches to form an almost solid canopy. The dense shade gave relief from the heat for about a hundred yards, then he drove out into the sunlight and there the ramp was, down a shallow slope that curved back to the right and was hidden from view by the thick trees until that moment.

He spun the wheel and headed down the slope,

the rear end of the Jeep slewing around before he deftly corrected. A blue Toyota pickup, with an empty boat trailer hooked to it, was pulled to the side. Another truck, a red extended-cab Chevy, was backed onto the ramp, and Charlotte Watkins was standing on the bank, one hand holding the rope to a long, sleek, red and silver fishing boat and the other hand slapping at mosquitoes as they swarmed around her bare arms and legs.

Jackson grabbed his shotgun and Kevlar vest and vaulted out of the Cherokee. "Thanks, Mrs. Watkins," he said as he took the rope from her. He put his right foot on the nose of the boat and pushed off with his left, agilely transferring his weight back to his right foot and stepping up into the boat as it floated away from the bank.

"Any time, Sheriff," she said, raising her hand to shade her eyes from the sun. "Mind the snags, now. If you get too far to the left, there are some mighty big stumps just under the water, and they'll rip the lower unit right off the boat."

"I'll watch," he promised as he carefully stowed the shotgun so it wouldn't bounce around, then slid into the driver's seat and hooked the kill switch to his shirt. As an afterthought, he tossed her the keys to his Jeep. "Drive the Cherokee home. I'll bring your truck and boat back as soon as I can."

She deftly caught the keys, but waved off any concern about the boat. "You just be careful upriver. I hope everything's all right." Worry etched her face.

Jackson turned the ignition switch and the big outboard coughed into deep, rumbling life. He put it in reverse and backed away from the bank, turning the boat so he was headed upriver. Then he pushed the throttle down and the nose of the boat rose out of the water as it gained speed, before dropping down and settling on the plane, skimming across the water.

The river was slow-moving and marshy, filled with snags, shoals, and weed beds ready to snare anyone unfamiliar with its obstacles. Mindful of Charlotte Watkins's warning—another woman who seemed to know an awful lot about the way to the Jones place—Jackson kept the boat dead center and prayed as he tried to balance urgency with caution, but urgency kept getting the upper hand. Maybe Miss Jones was having a peaceful summer afternoon, but maybe she wasn't.

The rush of air cooled him, drying the sweat on his body and making the thick heat of summer feel almost comfortable. As he skimmed past the little sloughs and cuts in the river he looked at all of them, hoping to see Thaniel doing nothing more sinister than feeding worms to the fish. No such luck.

Then he rounded a bend in the river and saw a flat-bottom boat pulled up on the bank and tied to a tree. Thaniel was nowhere in sight.

Jackson didn't slow. The Jones place couldn't be much farther up the river, because it looked as if Thaniel had decided to walk the rest of the way, so he could approach unnoticed. That gave Jackson a little more time, maybe enough time to head off any trouble.

Even as he had the thought he heard the shot, a deep report that boomed out over the water and was easily audible over the sound of the outboard motor. Shotgun, he thought. He eased up on the throttle and reached for the Kevlar vest, slipping it on and fastening the Velcro straps. Then he shoved the throttle down again, the boat leaping forward in response.

Fifteen seconds later the house was in sight,

taking form dead ahead of him, just as Jo had said. The river seemed to end right there. The house was built of old, weathered wood that blended into the tall trees surrounding it, but in front of it was a short dock with an old flat-bottom tied to it, and that was what he saw first.

He had to back off the power to bring the boat into the dock. He reached for his shotgun as he did, holding it in his left hand as he steered the boat. "This is Sheriff Brody!" he bellowed. "Thaniel, you stop whatever the hell it is you're doing and get your ass out here." Not the most professional way of speaking, he supposed, but it served the purpose of announcing him and letting Thaniel know his identity wasn't a secret.

But he didn't really expect things to settle down just because he was there, and they didn't. Another shotgun blast boomed, answered by the flatter crack of a rifle.

The shots were coming from the back of the house. Jackson nosed the boat toward the dock and killed the engine. He leaped out while the dock was still a foot away, automatically looping the mooring rope around one of the posts as he did so, ingrained training taking hold so everything was accomplished while he was in motion.

He ran up the short dock, the thudding of his boots on the wood in time with the hard beating of his heart. The old familiar clarity swept over him, the by-product of adrenaline and experience. He'd felt the same thing every time he jumped out of a plane during airborne training. Lightning-fast, his brain processed the details he saw.

The front door of the old wooden house was standing open, a neatly patched screen door keeping out the insects. He could see straight through to the back door, but no one was in sight. The porch looked like a jungle, with huge potted plants and hanging baskets everywhere, but there wasn't any junk sitting around like there was at most houses, his included. He took with one leap the three steps up to the porch, and flattened himself against the wall.

The last thing he wanted was to get shot by the very person he was trying to help, so he repeated his identity. "This is Sheriff Brody! Miss Jones, are you all right?"

There was a moment of silence in which even the insects seemed to stop buzzing. Then a woman's voice came from somewhere out back. "I'm fine. I'll be even better when you get this jackass off my property."

She sounded remarkably cool for someone who was under attack, as if Thaniel was of no more importance than the mosquitoes.

Jackson eased around the corner of the wide, shady porch that wrapped around three sides of the house. He was now on the right side, with thick woods both to the right and ahead of him. He couldn't see anything out of the ordinary, not a patch of color or a rustling of bushes. "Thaniel!" he yelled. "Put your weapon down before you get your stupid ass shot off, you hear me?"

There was another moment of silence. Then came a sullen, "I didn't do nothin', Sheriff. She shot at me first."

He still couldn't see Thaniel, but the voice had come from a stand of big pine trees behind the house, practically dead ahead. "I'll decide whose fault it is." He edged closer to the back of the house, his shotgun held ready. He was safe from Miss Jones's shots, for the moment, but Thaniel would have a straight bead on him if he chose. "Now do what I told you and pitch out your weapon."

"This crazy bitch will shoot me if I do."

"No, she won't."

"I might," came Delilah Jones's calm voice, not helping the situation at all.

"See, what'd I tell you!" Thaniel's voice was high with anxiety. Whatever he had planned, it had gone sadly awry.

Jackson swore under his breath, and tried to make his tone both calming and authoritative. "Miss Jones, where exactly are you?"

"I'm on the back porch, behind the washing machine."

"Put down your weapon and go back inside, so I can have a little talk with Thaniel."

Again that little pause, as if she were considering whether or not to pay any attention to him. Accustomed to instant response, be it positive or negative, that telling little hesitation set Jackson's teeth on edge. "I'll go in the house," she finally said. "But I'm not putting this shotgun down until that fool's off my property."

He'd had enough. "Do as you're told," he said sharply. "Or I'll arrest both of you."

There was another of those maddening moments of silence, then the back door slammed. Jackson took a deep breath. Thaniel's whiny voice floated from the pine trees. "She didn't put down the shotgun like you told her to, Sheriff."

"Neither did you," Jackson reminded him in a grim tone. He eased to the corner of the house. "I have a shotgun, too, and I'm going to use it in three seconds if you don't throw down that rifle and come out." The mood he was in, it wasn't a bluff. "One . . . two . . . th—"

A rifle sailed out from behind a huge pine tree, landing with a thud on the pine-needle-cushioned ground. After a few seconds, Thaniel slowly followed it, easing away from the tree with his hands up and his face sullen. A thin rivulet of blood ran down his right cheek. The wound didn't look like anything from a shotgun, so Jackson figured a splinter must have caught him. The tree trunk sported a great raw gouge level with his chin. Miss Jones hadn't been shooting over Thaniel's head; she had been aiming for him. And, from the look of that tree, she wasn't shooting bird shot.

Immediately the back screen door popped

open and Delilah Jones stepped out, shotgun held ready. Thaniel hit the ground, braying in panic. He covered his head with his hands, as if that would do any good.

God, give me strength, Jackson prayed. The prayer didn't do any good. His temper shattered and he moved fast, so fast she didn't have time to do more than glance at him, certainly not time to react. In two long steps he reached her, his right hand locking around the barrel of her shotgun and wrenching it out of her hands. "Get back inside," he barked. *"Now!"*

She stood as rigid as a post, staring at Thaniel, paying Jackson no more mind than if he hadn't been there at all. "You're dead," she said to Thaniel, her voice flat and calm.

Thaniel jerked as if he'd been shot. "You heard her!" he howled. "She threatened me, Sheriff! Arrest her!"

"I'm of a mind to do just that," Jackson said between clenched teeth.

"I didn't threaten him," she said, still in that flat, monotonous tone. "I don't have to. He'll die without me lifting a finger to help." She looked up at Jackson then, and he found himself caught in

144

eyes the dark green of a woodland forest, watchful, wary, knowing eyes.

He felt suddenly dizzy, and gave a short, sharp
jerk of his head. The heat must be getting to him.
Everything kind of faded, except her face at the
center of his vision. She was younger than he'd
expected, he thought dimly, probably in her late
twenties when he had expected a middle-aged,
reclusive country woman, bypassed by modern
inventions. Her skin was smooth, tanned, and
unblemished. Her hair was a mass of brown curls,
and her shorts stopped north of mid-thigh, revealing slim, shapely legs. He inhaled deeply, fighting
off the dizziness, and as his head cleared he
noticed that she had gone utterly white. She was
staring at him as if he had two heads.

Abruptly she turned and went inside, the
screen door slamming shut behind her.

Jackson took a deep breath, gathering himself
before turning back to the problem at hand. He
propped her shotgun against the wall and cradled
his on one arm as he finally turned his attention
back to Thaniel.

"Son of a *bitch!*"

Thaniel had taken advantage of his splintered

attention. The ground where he had lain was bare, and a quick glance told Jackson the rifle was gone, too.

He jumped off the porch, landing half-crouched, the shotgun now held ready in both hands. His head swiveled, but except for a slight waving of some bushes there was no sign of Thaniel. Silently Jackson slipped into the woods close to where the bushes swayed, then stood still and listened.

Thaniel, for all his other faults, was good in the woods. It was about thirty seconds before Jackson heard the distant snap of a twig under a careless foot. He started to follow, then stopped. There was no point in chasing him through the woods; he knew where Thaniel lived, if Miss Jones wanted to file charges against him for trespass and any other charges Jackson thought were applicable.

He turned and looked back at the house, nestled among the trees and blending in so well it looked part of the woodland. He felt oddly reluctant to go in and talk to Miss Jones, a sense of things being subtly altered, out of control. He didn't want to know anything more about her, he only wanted to get in Jerry Watkins's boat and go back downriver, safely away from that strange woman with her spooky eyes.

But his job demanded he talk to her, and Jackson was a good sheriff. That was why he was here, and that was why he couldn't leave without seeing her.

The uneasy feeling followed him, though, all the way to the porch.

3

The washing machine she'd been hiding behind was an old-fashioned wringer-type model, he noticed with faint astonishment as he paused in front of the screen door. He couldn't see inside the house; there were no lights on, and the trees provided plenty of shade to keep the interior cool and dim.

He lifted his fist to knock, paused, then gave two firm taps. "Miss Jones?"

"Right here."

She was near, standing in the room just beyond the door. There was a strained quality to her voice that hadn't been there before.

She hadn't asked him to come in. He was glad,

because he would just as soon never set foot in that house. And then, irrationally, it annoyed him that she hadn't asked him in. Without waiting for an invitation, he opened the screen door and stepped inside.

She was a pale figure in the dim room, standing very still, and staring at him. Maybe his vision needed to adjust a bit more, but he had the impression she was downright horrified by him. She even backed up a step.

He couldn't say why that pissed him off, but it did, big-time. Adrenaline was pumping through him again, making his muscles feel tight and primed for action, but damned if he knew what he could do. He had to take her statement, read her the riot act about shooting at people, and leave. That was all. Nothing there to make him feel so edgy and angry.

But that was exactly how he *did* feel, whether or not there was rhyme or reason to it.

Silence stretched between them, silence in which they took each other's measure. He didn't know what conclusions she drew from his appearance, but he was a lawman, accustomed to taking in every detail about a person and making snap judgments. He had to, and he had to be pretty accurate, because his and others' lives depended on how he read people.

What he saw in the dim light was a slim, toned young woman, neat in a pale yellow, sleeveless shirt that was tucked into khaki shorts, which were snugly belted around a trim waist. Her bare arms were smoothly tanned, and sleekly muscled in a feminine way that told him she was stronger than she looked, and accustomed to work. She was clean, even her bare feet—which, he noticed, sported pale pink polish on the toes; toes that were curling, digging into the floor, as if she had to force herself to stand there.

Her hair was a brown, sun-streaked mass of curls. She didn't hurt the eye, though she wasn't beauty-queen material. She was pleasant-looking, healthy, with a sweet curve to her chin. Her eyes, though . . . those eyes were spooky. He was reluctant to meet them again, but finally he did. They were her best feature, large and clear, fringed with thick dark lashes. And she was watching him now with . . . resignation?

For God's sake, what did she think he was going to do?

He didn't know how long he'd been standing there staring at her. The same thing had happened on the porch, only this time he didn't feel dizzy. He needed to take care of business and get going. The summer days were long, but he wanted to be off the river well ahead of sundown.

"Thaniel slipped away," he said, his voice unaccountably rough.

She gave a brief, jerky nod.

"Do you make a habit of shooting at visitors?"

The green eyes narrowed. "When they stop downriver and sneak the rest of the way on foot, yes, that makes me a bit suspicious about their reason for calling on me."

"How do you know what he did?"

"Sound carries a long way over water. And I don't hear many boats coming my way except Harley Whisenant's, delivering the mail. Since Harley was here this morning, I knew it wasn't him."

"You shot first."

"He was trespassing. I fired in the air the first time, as a warning, and yelled at him to scat. He shot at me then. There's a bullet hole in my washing machine, damn him. My second shot was to defend myself."

151

"Maybe he thought he was defending himself, too, since you shot first."

She gave him a disbelieving look. "He sneaked onto my property, up to my house, carrying a deer rifle, and when I yell at him to leave he fires from cover, and that's *defending* himself?"

He didn't know why he was giving her a hard time, except for the edginess that had him as prickly as a cactus. "You're right," he said abruptly.

"Well, thank you so much."

He ignored the sarcasm. "I need to take a statement."

"I'm not going to press charges."

She couldn't have picked anything to say more likely to rile him. In his opinion, a good deal of additional harm was done because people declined to bring charges against criminal actions. Whatever their reasoning, they didn't want to "cause trouble," or they wanted to give the perp "another chance." In his experience all they were doing was letting a criminal go free to commit another crime. There were circumstances that called for a little mercy, but this wasn't one of them. Thaniel Vargas wasn't a teenager caught on his first misdemeanor; he was a thug who had intended serious harm to another person.

"I beg your pardon?" He said it softly, reining in his inclination to roar, giving her a chance to rethink the situation. When he'd been a sergeant in the Army, enlisted men had immediately recognized that softness for the danger sign it was.

Either Delilah Jones wasn't as attuned to his mood as his men had been, or she wasn't impressed by his authority. Whatever the reason, she shrugged. "There's no point in it."

"No point?"

She started to say something, then stopped and gave a slight shake of her head. "It doesn't matter," she said, as if to herself. She bit her lip. He had the impression she was arguing with herself. She sighed. "Sit down, Sheriff Brody. You'll feel better after you've had something to eat."

He didn't want to sit down, he just wanted to get out of here. If she wasn't going to press charges, fine. He didn't agree, but the decision was hers. There was no reason for him to stay a minute longer.

But she was moving quietly and efficiently around the old-timey kitchen, slicing what looked

153

like homemade bread, then thick slices from a ham, and a big chunk of cheese. She dipped a glass of water from a bucket, and placed the simple meal on the table.

Jackson watched her with narrowed eyes. Despite himself, he admired the deft, feminine way she did things, without fuss or bother. She made herself a sandwich, too, though not as thick as his, and minus the cheese. She sat down across from the place she had set for him, and lifted her eyebrows in question at his hesitancy.

The sight of that sandwich made his mouth water. He was so hungry his stomach was churning. That was why he removed the Kevlar vest and set the shotgun aside, then sat down and put his boots under her table. Without a word they both began to eat.

The ham was succulent, the cheese mellow. He finished the sandwich before she had taken more than a few bites of hers. She got up and began making another one for him. "No, one was plenty—" he lied, not wanting to put her to any more trouble, not wanting to stay any longer.

"I should have thought," she said, her voice low. "I'm not used to feeding a big man like you.

Pops was a skinny little thing; he didn't eat much more than I do."

In thirty seconds another thick sandwich was set down in front of him. She sat down again and picked up her own sandwich.

He ate more slowly this time, savoring the tastes. As he chewed, he took stock of his surroundings. Something about this house bothered him, and now he realized what it was: the silence. There was no refrigerator humming, no television squawking in the background, no water heater thumping and hissing.

He looked around. There was no refrigerator, period. No lamps. No overhead lights. She had dipped the water from a bucket. He looked at the sink; there were no faucets. The evidence was all there, but he still asked, "You don't have electricity?" because it was so unbelievable that she didn't.

"No."

"No phone, no way of calling for help if you need it?"

"No. I've never needed help."

"Until today."

"I could have handled Thaniel. He's been trying to bully me since grade school."

"Has he ever come after you with a gun before?"

"Not that I remember, but then I don't pay much attention to him."

She was maddening. He wanted to shake her, wanted to put his hands on those bare arms and shake her until her teeth rattled. "You're lucky you weren't raped and murdered," he snapped.

"It wasn't luck," she corrected. "It was preparation."

Despite himself, he was interested. "What sort of preparation?"

She leaned back in her chair, looking around at the silent house. It struck Jackson that she was very comfortable here, alone in the woods, without any of the modern conveniences everyone else thought they had to have. "To begin with, this is my home. I know every inch of the woods, every weed bed in the river. If I had to hide, Thaniel would never find me."

Watching her closely, Jackson saw the secret smile lurking in her green eyes and he knew, as sure as he knew his own name, that she doubted she would ever be reduced to hiding. "What about the other stuff?" he asked, keeping his tone casual.

She gave him a slow smile, and he got the feeling she was pleased with his astuteness. "Oh, just a few little things that give me advance warning. There's nothing lethal out there, unless you step on a water moccasin or fall in the water and drown."

He stared at her mouth, and felt a little jolt, like another kick of adrenaline. Despite the coolness of the house he broke out in a light sweat. God almighty, he hoped she didn't smile again. Her smile was sleepy and sexy, womanly, the kind of smile a woman gave a man after they had made love, lying drowsy on tangled sheets while the rain beat down outside and there were only the two of them, cocooned in their private world.

The sexual awareness wasn't welcome. He had to be careful in situations like this. He was a man in a position of authority, alone with a woman to whose house he had gone in an official capacity. This wasn't the time or the place to come on to her.

Silence had fallen again, silence in which they faced each other across the table. She took a deep breath, and the inhalation lifted her breasts against the thin cotton of her blouse. Her nipples were plainly outlined, hard and erect, the darkness of the aureolas faintly visible where they pressed against the fabric. Was she cold, or aroused?

The skin on her arms was smooth; no chill bumps.

"I'd better go," he said, fighting the sudden thickness in his throat, and in his pants. "Thank you for the sandwiches. I was starving."

She looked both relieved and reluctant. "You're welcome. You had that hungry look, so I—" She stopped, and waved a dismissive hand. "Never mind. I was glad to have the company. And you're right about going; if I'm not mistaken, I heard thunder just a minute ago." She got up and gathered their glasses, taking them to the sink.

He got up, too. There was something about her unfinished sentence that pulled at him. He should have let it go, should have said good-bye and got into the boat and left. He hadn't heard any thunder, though his hearing was pretty good, but that was as good an excuse as any to get the hell out of there. He knew it, and still he said, "So you— what?"

Her gaze slid away from him, as if she were embarrassed. "So I . . . thought you must have missed lunch."

How would she know that? Why would she even think it? He didn't normally miss a meal, and how in hell would she know if he looked hungry or not, when she had never seen him before today? For all she knew, ill-tempered was his normal expression.

Witch. The word whispered in his mind, even though he knew it was nonsense. Even if he believed in witchcraft, which he didn't, from what he'd read it had nothing to do with telling whether or not a man had missed lunch. She had noticed he was grouchy, and attributed it to an empty stomach. He didn't quite follow the reasoning, but he'd often seen his mother ply his father with food to gentle him out of a bad mood. It was a woman thing, not a witch thing.

"Meow."

He almost jumped a foot in the air. Now was *not* the time to find out she had a cat.

"There you are," she crooned, looking down at his feet. He looked down too, and saw a huge, fluffy white cat with black ears and a black tail, rubbing against his right boot.

159

"Poor kitty," she said, still crooning, and leaned down to pick up the creature, holding it in her arms as if it were a baby. It lay perfectly relaxed, belly up, eyes half-closed in a beatific expression as she rubbed its chest. "Did the noise scare you? The bad man's gone, and he won't bother us again, I promise." She looked up at Jackson. "Eleanor's pregnant. The kittens are due any time now, I think. She showed up about a week ago, but she's obviously tame and has had good care, so I guess someone just drove into the country and put her out, rather than take care of a litter."

The cat looked like a feline Buddha, fat and content. Familiars were supposed to be black, weren't they, or would any cat do, even fat white pregnant ones?

He couldn't resist reaching out and stroking that fat, round belly. The cat's eyes completely closed and she began purring so loudly, she sounded like a motor idling.

Delilah smiled. "Careful, or you'll have a slave for life. Maybe you'd like to take her with you?"

"No, thanks," he said dryly. "My mother might like a kitten, though. Her old tom died last year and she doesn't have a pet now."

"Check back in six or seven weeks, then."

That wasn't exactly an invitation to come calling anytime soon, he thought. He picked up the shotgun and vest. "I'll be on my way, Miss Jones. Thanks again for the sandwiches."

"Lilah."

"What?"

"Please call me Lilah. All my friends do." She gave him a distinctly warning look. "*Not* Delilah, please."

He chuckled. "Message received. I guess you got teased about it in school?"

"You have no idea," she said feelingly.

"My name's Jackson."

"I know." She smiled. "I voted for you. Jackson's a nice Texas-sounding name."

"I'm a nice Texas guy."

She made a noncommittal sound, as if she didn't agree with him but didn't want to come right out and say so. He grinned as he turned to the door. Meeting Delilah Jones had been interesting. He didn't know if it was good, but it was definitely interesting. The blue-moon mojo was at full strength today. When things settled down and he had time to think things over, when he could be entirely rational about the weirdness and come up with a logical explanation, maybe he'd come back to visit—and not in any official capacity.

"Use the front door," she said. "It's closer."

He followed her through the small house. From what he could tell there were only four rooms: the kitchen and living room on one side, and each of those had another room opening off it. He figured the other two rooms were bedrooms. The living room was simply furnished with a couch and a rocking chair, arranged around a rag rug spread in front of the stone fireplace. Oil lamps sat on the mantel and on the pair of small tables set beside the couch and chair. In one corner was a treadle sewing machine. A handmade quilt hung on one of the walls, a brightly colored scene of trees and water that must have taken forever to do. On another wall a bookcase—also handmade, from the looks of it—stretched from floor to ceiling, and was packed with books, both hardback and paper.

The whole house made him feel as if he had stepped back a century, or at least half of one. The only modern appliance he saw was a battery-operated weather radio, sitting beside one of the oil lamps on the mantel. He was glad she had it; both tornadoes and hurricanes were possible in this area.

He stepped out on the porch, Lilah right behind him, still holding the cat. He stopped dead still, staring at the dock. "The son of a bitch," he said softly.

"What?" She pushed at his shoulder, and he realized he was blocking her view.

"The boats are gone," he said, stepping aside so she could see.

She stared at the empty dock, too, her green eyes wide with dismay. Her flat-bottom was gone, as well as Jerry Watkins's bass boat.

"He must have doubled back and cut the boats loose while we were eating. They can't have drifted far. If I walk along the bank, I'll probably find them."

"My boat had oars in it," she said. "I always have them in case I have motor trouble. He didn't have to cut them loose, he could have rowed mine out, and towed yours. That would save him the trouble of hiking back to his boat, and once he got to his boat he'd probably let the current take them. I figure they're at least a mile downstream by now, maybe more. That's if he doesn't decide to sink them."

"I'll call in—" he began, the notion so automatic that the words were out before he realized he didn't have his radio. He didn't have his cell phone. They were both in the Cherokee, which Charlotte Watkins had driven home. And Lilah Jones didn't have a phone.

He looked down at her. "I don't suppose you have a shortwave radio?"

"Afraid not." She was staring grimly at the river down which her boat had vanished, as if she could will it back. "You're stuck here. We both are."

"Not for long. The dispatcher—"

"Jo?"

"Jo." He wondered how well she knew Jo. Jo hadn't talked as if they were anything more than distant acquaintances, but Lilah not only knew who his dispatcher was, she had called her Jo instead of Jolene, which was her given name. "She knows where I am, and she was supposed to send backup as soon as some was available. A deputy should be along anytime."

"Not unless he's already on his way," she said. "Look." She pointed to the southwest.

Jackson looked, and swore under his breath. A huge purplish black thunderhead had filled the late-afternoon sky. He could feel its breath now in the freshening wind that fanned him, hear its voice in the sullen bass rumble of thunder as it marched toward them.

"A thunderstorm probably won't last long." At least he hoped it wouldn't. The way things were going today, the storm's forward progress would stop just as it was on top of them.

She was staring worriedly at the cloud. "I think I'd better turn on the weather radio," she said, and went back inside, Eleanor cradled in her arms.

Jackson gave the empty river another frustrated glance. The air felt charged with electricity, raising the hair on his arms. The blade of lightning slashed down, flickering and flashing, and thunder rumbled again.

He was stuck here for at least a few hours, and maybe all night. If he had to be stuck anywhere, why couldn't it be in his own home? There was always a rash of accidents on a stormy night, and the deputies would need him.

Instead he would be here, in a house in the back of nowhere, keeping company with a witch and her pregnant cat.

4

Lilah put Eleanor on the floor and turned on the weather radio, then went into her bedroom, which opened off the living room, and pulled down the side window. The front window was protected by the wide porch, so rain wasn't likely to come in there. With an ear cocked toward the radio, she then did the same in the back bedroom. She knew that Sheriff Brody had come in from the porch, but she deliberately ignored him, doing what needed to be done. He was entirely too big for her small house, too stern, too authoritative, too . . . too *male.*

He disrupted her peaceful life far more than

Thaniel Vargas had ever dreamed of doing. What on earth had Jo been thinking, sending him out here? But of course Jo didn't know, and she had, rightly, been worried about Thaniel.

Well, poor Thaniel wouldn't be bothering her again, and there was nothing she could do about it. If he hadn't run she might have—well, whether or not she could have helped him was a moot point, because it was too late now. Still, regret filled her. Whatever Thaniel's faults—and they were many—she didn't wish him any harm. And though she would have tried to help if . . . if he hadn't run away, years of painful experience had taught her there was very little she could do to alter fate.

That was why the sheriff filled her with such panic. She had known, the moment she saw him, that he was fated to destroy her safe, comfortable, familiar life. She wanted to get as far away from him as she could, she wanted to push him out of her house and lock the door, she wanted . . . she wanted to walk into his arms and rest her head on a broad shoulder, let him hold her and kiss her and do anything else he wanted to her.

In all her life she'd never met a male, boy or

man, who elicited even the slightest sexual response on her part. She had always felt isolated from the rest of the world, forever alone because of what she was. The thought of spending her life alone hadn't bothered her; quite the opposite. She enjoyed her solitude, her life, her sense of completion within herself. So many people never achieved wholeness, and spent their entire lives searching for someone or something to make them whole, never realizing that the answer was within themselves. She liked her own company, she trusted her own decisions, and she enjoyed the work she did. There was nothing—*nothing*—in her life that she wanted changed.

But Jackson Brody changed everything, whether she wanted him to or not.

It wasn't just his aura that attracted her, though it was so rich she was almost spellbound by it. All his colors were clear: the dark red of sensuality, the blue of calm, the turquoise of a dynamic personality, the orange of power, with fluctuating spikes of spiritual purple and yellow, healing green. Nothing about him was murky. He was a straightforward, confident, healthy man.

What had so stunned her, however, was the

sudden flash of precognition. She didn't have them often; her particular talent was her ability to see auras. But sometimes she had lightning bursts of insight and knowledge, and she had never been wrong. Not once. Just as she had looked at Thaniel and known he would soon die, when she first focused on Jackson Brody the wave of precognition had been so strong she had almost slumped to her knees. This man would be her lover. This man would be her love, the only one of her life.

She didn't *want* a lover! She didn't want a man hanging around, getting in her way, interfering with her business. He would; she knew he would. He struck her as impatient, used to giving orders, slightly domineering, and, oh my, sexy as all get-out. He certainly wouldn't want to live out here, without any of the modern conveniences to which he was accustomed, while she much preferred her uncluttered life. She *felt* better without hustle and bustle, without electrical machines incessantly humming in the background. Nevertheless, he would undoubtedly expect her to move to town, or at least to someplace less isolated and more accessible.

Once he realized she couldn't be relocated, he

would give in, but with bad grace. He'd argue that he wouldn't be able to see her as often as he could if she lived closer. He would visit whenever it was convenient for him, and expect her to drop whatever she was doing whenever he pulled his boat up to the dock. In short, he would be very inconvenient for her, and there wasn't a damn thing she could do about it. For all the success she'd had in evading or altering fate, she might as well strip off her clothes right now and lead him into the bedroom.

That was another worry. She was rather short on experience in the bedroom department. That hadn't been a bother before, because she hadn't felt even an inkling of desire to get that experience. Now she did. Just looking at him made her feel warm and sort of breathless; her breasts tingled, and she had to press her thighs together to contain the hot ache between her legs. So this was lust. She had wondered, and now she knew. No wonder people acted like fools when they were afflicted with it.

If Thaniel hadn't stolen the boats, the sheriff would have already been gone, and she likely wouldn't have seen him again for quite a while, if

screen door. "Here it com... ...and she
turned her head to watch
upriver toward the hou
straight downward, and a
the windows.

Eleanor meowed, a
cardboard box which
towels as a bed for the

Jackson prowled
room. Lilah looked
dering if he ever ju
irritating to him th
er somehow, either
ing it speeding o
risk getting upriv

She gave a m
work to do.

The first sh
down on the
was almost c
rooms. She moved thro
lamps set on the mantel, her hand setti
the match box. The rasp of the match was unheard
in the din of rain, but he turned at the sudden
small bloom of light and watched as she lifted the

ever. She would have gone about her quiet, very satisfying life. But she should have expected that trick with the boats; how else could Fate have arranged for Jackson to stay here? And of course a storm was coming up, preventing any of his deputies from arriving. All of it was inevitable. No matter how inconceivable her visions, almost immediately there would set in motion a train of events that brought about the conclusion she had foreseen.

Not for the first time, she wished she wasn't different. She wished she didn't know things were going to happen before they did; that was asking a lot of a person. She couldn't regret seeing auras, though; her life would feel colorless and less interesting if she no longer saw them. She didn't have to speak to someone to know how he or she was feeling; she could *see* when someone was happy, or angry, or feeling ill. She could see bad intentions, dishonesty, meanness, but she could also see joy, and love, and goodness.

"Is something wrong?"

He was standing right behind her, and the sharpness of his tone told her she had been standing in one place, staring at nothing, for quite a

... she didn't blam[e] ... less than an hour ago, they w... whopper of a storm was bearing down on... that should be enough to keep her thoughts grounded. She should have said she was thinking, instead of daydreaming; at least that sounded pro-ductive.

"Never mind. Have there been any weather bulletins or warnings on the radio?"

"Severe thunderstorm warning until ten tonight. High winds, damaging hail."

Hours. They would be alone together for hours. He would probably be here until morning. What was she supposed to do with him, this man she was going to love but didn't yet? She had just met him, she knew nothing about him on a per-sonal level. She was attracted to him, yes, but love? Not likely. Not yet, anyway.

Fresh, rain-fragrant wind gusted through the

---

globes of the lamps and touched the match to the wicks, then replaced the globes. She blew out the match and tossed it into the fireplace.

Without a word she went into the kitchen and duplicated the chore, though there were four oil lamps there because she liked more light when she was working. The fire in the stove had been banked; she opened the door, stirred the hot coals, and added more wood.

"What are you doing?" he asked from the doorway.

Mentally she rolled her eyes. "Cooking." Maybe he'd never seen the process before.

"But we just ate."

"So we did, but those sandwiches won't hold you for long, if I'm any judge." She eyed him, measuring him against the doorframe. A little over six feet tall, she guessed, and at least two hundred pounds. He looked muscled, given the way his shoulders filled out his shirt, so he might weigh more. This man would eat a lot.

He came on into the room and settled at the table, turning the chair around so he faced her, his long legs stretched out and crossed at the ankle. His fingers drummed on the table. "This irritates the hell out of me," he confessed.

Her tone was dry. "I noticed." She dipped some water into the washbowl and washed her hands.

"Usually I can do *something*. Usually, in bad weather, I *have* to do something, whether it's working a wreck or dragging people off of flooded roads. I need to be out there now, because my deputies will have their hands full."

So that was the cause of his restlessness and irritability; he knew his help was needed, but he couldn't leave here. She liked his sense of responsibility.

He watched in silence then as she prepared her biscuit pan, spraying it with nonstick spray. She got her mixing bowl and scooped some flour into it, added shortening and buttermilk, and plunged her hands into the bowl.

"I haven't seen anyone do that in years." He smiled as he kept his eyes on her hands, deftly mixing and kneading. "My grandmother used to, but I can't remember ever seeing my mother make biscuits by hand."

"I don't have a refrigerator," she said practically. "Frozen biscuits are out."

"Don't you want to have things like refrigerators and electric stoves? Doesn't it bother you, not having electricity?"

"Why should it? I don't depend on a wire for heat and light. If I had electricity, the power might be off right now and I wouldn't be able to cook."

He rubbed his jaw, brow furrowed as he thought. She liked the sight, she mused, eyeing him as she continued to knead. His brows were straight and dark, nicely shaped. Everything about him was nicely shaped. She bet that all the single women in town, and a few of the married ones, were hot for him. Short dark hair, bright blue eyes, strong jaw, soft lips—she didn't know how she knew his lips were soft, but she did. Oh, yeah, they were hot for him. She was a bit warm herself.

She thought of walking over to him and straddling his lap, and an instantaneous flush swept over her entire body. Warm, my foot; she thought she might break out in a sweat any minute now.

"Running a gas line would be even harder than running power lines," he mused, his mind still on the issue of modern conveniences. "I guess you could get a propane tank, but filling it would be a bitch, since there aren't any roads out here."

"The wood stove suits me fine. It's only a few

years old, so it's very efficient. It heats the whole house, and it's easy to regulate." She began pinching off balls of dough and rolling them between her hands, shaping them into biscuits and placing them in the pan. If she kept her eyes on the dough, instead of him, the hot feeling cooled down somewhat.

"Where do you get your wood?"

She couldn't help it. She had to look at him, her expression incredulous. "I cut it myself." Where did he think she got it? Maybe he thought the wood fairies chopped it and piled it up for her.

To her surprise, he surged up out of the chair, looming over her with a scowl. "Chopping wood is too hard for you."

"Gee, I'm glad you told me, otherwise I'd have kept doing it and not known any better." She edged away from him, turning to the sink to wash the dough from her hands.

"I didn't mean you couldn't do it, I meant you shouldn't have to," he growled. His voice was right behind her. *He* was right behind her. Without warning, he reached around her and wrapped his fingers around her right wrist. His hand completely engulfed hers. "Look at that. My wrist is twice as thick as yours. You may be strong for your size, but you can't tell me it isn't a struggle for you to chop wood."

"I manage." She wished he hadn't touched her. She wished he wasn't standing so close that she could feel the heat from his body, smell the hot man-smell of him.

"And it's dangerous. What if the ax slips, or the saw, or whatever you use? You're out here alone, a long way from medical help."

"A lot of things are dangerous." She struggled to keep her voice practical, and even. "But people do what they have to do, and I have to have wood." Why hadn't he released her hand? Why hadn't she pulled it away herself? She could; he wasn't holding her tightly. But she liked the feel of his hand wrapped around hers, liked the warmth and strength, the roughness of the calluses on his palm.

"I'll chop it for you," he said abruptly.

"What!" She almost turned around; common sense stopped her at the last minute. If she turned around, she would be face-to-face, belly to belly, with him. She didn't dare. She swallowed. "You can't chop my wood."

"Why not?"

"Because—" Because, why? "Because you won't be here."

"I'm here now." He paused, and his tone dropped lower. "I can be again."

She went still. The only sound was the storm, the boom of thunder and wind lashing through the trees, the rain pounding down on the roof. Or maybe it was her heart, pounding against her rib cage.

"I have to be careful here," he said quietly. "I'm acting as a man, not a sheriff. If you tell me no, I'll go back to the table and sit down. I'll keep my distance from you for the rest of the night, and I won't bother you again. But if you don't tell me no, I'm going to kiss you."

Lilah inhaled, fighting for oxygen. She couldn't say a word, couldn't think of anything to say even if she had the air. She was feeling hot again, and weak, as if she might collapse against him.

"I'll take that as a yes," he said, and turned her into his arms.

5

His lips were soft, just the way she'd known they would be. And he was gentle, rather than bruising her lips by pressing too hard. He didn't try to overwhelm her with a sudden display of passion. He simply kissed her, taking his time about it, tasting her and learning the shape and texture of her own lips. The leisurely pace was more seductive than anything else he could have done.

She sighed, a low hum of pleasure, and let herself relax against him. He gathered her up, wrapping his arms around her and lifting her onto her toes so that they fit together more intimately. The full press of his body against her made her catch her breath, and that now-familiar wave of heat swept over her again. She looped her arms around his neck, pressing even closer, shivering a little as his tongue moved slowly into her mouth, giving her time to pull away if she didn't want such a deep kiss. She did, more than she had ever thought she would want a man's kiss.

Her heart thudded wildly in her chest. Pleasure was a siren, luring her to experience more, to take everything he could give her. His erection was a hard ridge in his pants; she wanted to rub herself against it, open herself to it. Knowing herself to be on the verge of losing control, she forced herself to pull away from the slow, intoxicating kisses, burying her face instead in the warm column of his throat.

He wasn't unaffected. His pulse hammered through his veins; she felt it, there in his neck, just where her lips rested. His lungs pumped, dragging in air. His skin felt hot and damp, and he moved restlessly, as if he wanted to grind his hips against her.

He didn't say anything, for which she was grateful. Innate caution told her to slow down, while instinct screamed at her, urging her to mate with him; it was fated, anyway, so why wait?

What would waiting accomplish? The outcome was the same, no matter the timetable. Torn between the two, she hesitated, not quite willing yet to take such a large step no matter what the fates said.

"This is scary," she muttered against his throat.

"No joke." He buried his face against her hair. "This must be what it feels like to get hit by that famous ton of bricks."

The knowledge that he was as rattled as she wasn't very reassuring, because she would have liked for one of them to be in control.

"We don't know each other." Neither did she know with whom she was arguing, him or herself. All she knew was that, for one of the few times in her life, she wasn't certain of herself. She didn't like the feeling. One of the foundation bricks of her life, her very self, was her knowledge of herself and other people; *not* to know was if that foundation was being shaken.

"We'll work on that." His lips brushed her temple. "We don't have to rush into anything."

But when he *did* know her, would he still want her? She worried at that, feeling, not for the first time, the weight of her differentness. She came with so much excess baggage that a lot of men would think she was more trouble than she was worth.

That thought gave her the strength to push gently at his shoulders. He released her immediately, stepping back. Lilah took a deep breath and pushed her hair out of her face, trying not to look at him, but the clear, dark red of passion emanating from him was almost impossible to ignore. "I'd better get those biscuits in the oven," she said, stepping around him. "Just sit down out of my way and I'll have supper ready in a jiffy."

"I'll stand, thank you," he said wryly.

She couldn't help it; she had to look, meeting his rueful blue gaze in perfect understanding. The dark red of his aura was still glowing hot and clear, especially in the groin area, though more blue was beginning to show through in the aura around his head.

But he did move out of her way, leaning against the wall by the door. She put the biscuits into the oven and opened a big can of beef stew, dumping the contents into a pot and placing that on top of the stove. The simple meal would have to be enough, because she wasn't about to go out into the storm to chase down a chicken for supper. The biscuits could cool, and the beef stew could simmer until he got hungry again.

He was watching her. She felt his gaze, his utter male focus on her. Being female wasn't something to which she gave a great deal of thought, but under that intent study she was suddenly, acutely aware of her body, of the way her breasts lifted with each breath, of the folds between her legs where he would enter. She didn't have to look down to know her nipples were tightly beaded, or at the front of his pants to know his erection hadn't yet subsided.

His unabashed arousal did more to turn her on than any sweet nothing he could have whispered. Something had to be done to lessen the sensual tension, or she would shortly find herself on her back. She cleared her throat, mentally searching for a neutral topic.

"How did a nice Texas boy end up in Alabama?" She already knew; Jo had told her. But it was the only thing she could think of, and at least the question would get him to talking.

"My mother was from Dothan."

No further explanation followed. Deciding he

needed more prodding, Lilah said, "Why did she move to Texas?"

"She met my dad. He was from west Texas. Mom and a couple of friends from college were driving to California after graduation, and they had car trouble. My dad was a deputy then, and he stopped to help them. Mom never did get to California."

That was better; he was talking. She breathed an inner sigh of relief. "Why did she come back to Alabama, then?"

"Dad died a few years ago." He settled his shoulders more comfortably against the wall. "West Texas isn't for everyone; it can be hot as hell, and pretty damn empty. She never complained while Dad was alive, but after he died, the loneliness got to her. She wanted to move back to Alabama, close to her sister and her friends from college."

"So you came with her?"

"She's my mother," he said simply. "I can be in law enforcement here as easily as I could in Texas. Mom and I don't live together, haven't since I was eighteen and went away to college, but she knows I'm nearby if she needs anything."

"It didn't bother you at all to leave Texas?" She

couldn't imagine such a thing. She loved her home, knew it as intimately as she knew herself. She loved the scent of the river in the early mornings, the way it turned gold when the dawn light struck it, she loved the dramatic weather that produced violent thunderstorms and torrents of rain, the hot, humid days when even the birds seemed lethargic, and the gray winter days when a fire in the fireplace and a cup of hot soup were the best she could ask of life.

He shrugged. "Home is family, not a place. I've got some aunts and uncles in Texas, a whole herd of cousins, but no one as close to me as Mom. I can always visit Texas if I feel the need."

He loved his mother, and was unabashed about it. Lilah swallowed, hard. Her own mother had died when she was five, but she cherished the few memories she had of the woman who had been the center of life in the isolated little house.

"What about you?" he asked. "Are you from here originally?"

"I was born in this house. I've lived here all my life."

He gave her a quizzical look, and she knew what he was thinking. Most babies were born in a hospital, and had been for the last fifty years. She was obviously younger than that, but too old to have been part of the birth-at-home fashion that was making a comeback in some sections.

"Didn't your daddy have time to get her to the hospital?"

"She didn't want a hospital." Was now the time to explain that her mother had been a folk healer, like her? That she too had seen the bursts of color that surrounded people, and taught her daughter what they meant, how to read them? That she had known everything would be all right, and thus hadn't seen any purpose in spending their hard-earned money on a hospital and doctor she didn't need?

"That was one tough lady," he said, shaking his head. A small smile curved his mouth. "I delivered a baby when I was a rookie. Scared the hell out of me, and the mother wasn't too happy, either. But we got through it, and they were both okay." The smile turned into a grin. "My bedside manner must have been a tad off, though; she *didn't* name the baby after me. As I recall, her exact words were: 'No offense, but I never want to see you again for the rest of my life.' "

Lilah threw back her head on a gusty laugh. She could just see a young, inexperienced rookie deputy, sweating and panicky, delivering a baby. "What happened? Did the baby come early, or just fast?"

"Neither. West Texas does get snow, and that was one of the times. The roads were in really bad shape. She and her husband were on the way to the hospital, but their car slid off the road into a drift not a mile from their house, so they walked back home and called for help. I was in the area, and I had a four-wheel drive, but by the time I got to their house the weather was even worse, so bad I wouldn't risk the drive." He rubbed his ear. "She cussed me, called me every name I'd ever heard before, and a few that I hadn't. She wanted something for the pain, and I was the one keeping her from getting it, so she made sure I suffered right along with her."

His grin invited her to laugh at the image his words conjured. Lilah snickered as she checked on the biscuits. "What about her husband?"

"Useless. Every time he came around he got an even worse cussing than I did, so he stayed out of sight. I'm telling you, that was one unhappy lady."

"How long did her labor last?"

"Nineteen hours and twenty-four minutes," he promptly replied. "The longest nineteen hours and twenty-four minutes in the history of the world, according to her. She swore she'd been in labor at least three days."

Under the amusement in his tone was a thread of . . . joy. She tilted her head, wondering if she read him correctly. "You liked it." The words weren't quite a question.

He laughed. "Yeah, I did. It was exciting, and funny, and amazing as hell. I've seen puppies and calves and foals being born, but I've never felt anything like when that baby slid into my hands. By the way, it was a girl. Jackson just didn't seem to suit her."

His aura was glowing now with more green in the mixture, shot through with joyful yellow. Lilah no longer had to wonder when she would fall in love with him. She did in that moment, something inside her melting, growing hotter. She knew her own aura would be showing pink, and she blushed, even though she knew he couldn't see it.

She felt trembly, and had to sit down. This was momentous. She'd never thought she would love the way others did, not romantically. She loved many people and many things, but not like this. Always, mixed in with her feelings, was the knowledge that she was set apart from them, a caretaker rather than a partner. Even with Pops she'd been the rock on which he leaned. But Jackson was a strong man, both mentally and physically. He didn't need anyone to take care of him; rather, he did the caring.

If she hadn't been able to see his aura, she would eventually have loved him anyway. But she could see it, and she knew the essence of the man. That, and her own precognitive recognition of him as her mate, destroyed her sense of caution. She wanted to throw herself into his arms and let him do whatever he wanted. Instead she got up and checked the biscuits.

She stood there with the oven door open, letting heat escape, staring blindly at the biscuits. Jackson came up behind her. "Perfect," he said with approval.

She blinked. The biscuits were a golden brown, perfectly risen. She had a good hand with biscuits, or so Pops had always said. She took a deep breath and, using a dish cloth, took the hot pan out of the oven and set it on a cooling rack.

"Why does Vargas think you're a witch?"

That brought her to earth with a thud. The change in his tone was subtle, but there: He was the sheriff, and he wanted to know if anyone in his county was practicing witchcraft.

"Several reasons, I suppose." She turned to face him, her expression cool and unreadable. "I live alone out in the woods, I seldom go into town, I don't socialize. The witch rumor started when I was in fourth grade, I think."

"Fourth grade, huh?" He leaned against the cabinet, blue gaze sharp on her face. "I guess he'd been watching too many *Bewitched* reruns."

She lifted one eyebrow and waited.

"So you don't cast spells, or dance naked in the moonlight, or anything like that?"

"I'm not a witch," she said plainly. "I've never cast a spell, though I might dance naked in the moonlight, if the notion took me."

"Do tell." The gaze warmed, and moved slowly down her body. "Call me if you need a dancing partner."

"I'll do that."

He looked up, met her eyes, and as simply as that, there was no longer any need for caution.

"Are you hungry?" he asked, moving closer, stroking one finger up her bare arm.

"No."

"So the biscuits and beef stew can wait?"

"They can."

He took the dishcloth and set the pan of stew off the eye. "Will you go to bed with me, then, Lilah Jones?"

"I will."

6

Lilah lit the lamp in her bedroom and turned it low. The storm and heavy rain made the room as dark as night, lit briefly by the flashes of lightning. Jackson seemed to fill the small room, his shoulders throwing a huge shadow over the wall. His aura, visible even in the low light, pulsated with that deep, clear red again, the color of passion and sensuality.

He began unbuttoning his shirt, and she turned back the bedcovers, neatly folding the quilt and plumping the pillows. Her bed looked small, she thought, though it was a double. It was certainly too small for him. Perhaps she should see about getting a larger one, though she wasn't certain how long he would use hers. That was the problem with the flashes of precognition; they told her facts, but not circumstances. She knew only that Jackson would be her lover, and her love. She had no idea if he would love her in return, if they would be together forever or only this one time.

"You look nervous." Despite the sharpness of his desire, which she could plainly see, his voice was quiet. His shirt was unbuttoned but he hadn't yet removed it. Instead he was watching her, his cop's eyes seeing too much.

"I am," she admitted.

"If you don't want to do this, just say so. No hard feelings—well, except for one place," he said wryly.

"I do want to do this. That's why I'm nervous." Looking him in the eye, she unfastened her shorts and let them drop, then began unbuttoning her shirt. "I've never been so . . . attracted to anyone before. I'm always cautious, but—" She shook her head. "I don't want to be cautious with you."

He shrugged the shirt off and let it drop to the floor. Lamplight gleamed on his shoulders, delineating the smooth, powerful muscles, and the broad chest shadowed with dark hair. Lilah inhaled deeply through her nose, feeling the warmth of arousal spread through her. She forgot what she was doing, just stood there looking at him, greedily drinking in the sight of her man undressing.

He sat down on the edge of the bed and leaned forward to pull off his boots. Now she could admire the deep furrow of his spine, the rippling muscles in his back. Her heartbeat picked up in speed, and she got even warmer.

The boots thunked on the wooden floor. He stood and unfastened his pants, let them drop, and pushed down his shorts. Totally naked, he stepped out of the circle of clothing and turned to face her.

Oh, my.

She must have said the words aloud, breathing them in hunger and lust and maybe even some bit of fear, because he laughed as he came to her, brushing aside her stalled hands and finishing the job of unbuttoning her shirt. He put his hands inside the shirt and smoothed them over her shoulders and down her arms, slipping the shirt off so easily she scarcely knew when it left. She wasn't paying attention to her clothing anyway, only to the jutting penis that brushed her belly when he moved.

She wrapped her hands around it, lightly stroking, exploring, delighting in the heat and hardness and textures, so different from her own body. Now it was he who sucked in a breath, his eyes closing as he stilled for a moment. Then he moved even closer, pushing his hands inside her panties and gripping the globes of her bottom as he pulled her to him. She had to release his penis and she made a sound of . . . disappointment? Impatience? Both. But there was reward in the pressure of his hard, hairy chest on her breasts, in the rasping sensation to her nipples. Her entire body seemed to go boneless, melting into him, curving to fit his contours.

His breathing was ragged. "Let's get you naked so I can look at you," he muttered, releasing her bottom long enough to push her panties down her thighs. She wiggled until they dropped to her feet, and his breathing caught on a groan.

"God! You're a natural-born tease, aren't you?" He pulled her up on her toes, welding her to him.

"Am I?" She had never thought about teasing a man before, never wanted to; but if what she was doing was teasing him, then that was only fair, because she was driving herself crazy, too. The feel of their bare bodies brushing together was so delicious she wanted to moan. She kept moving against him, rubbing her nipples against his chest and turning them into hard, aching peaks.

He stroked his hands over her bottom and back, his hands so hot and rough she wanted to purr. Then one hand went lower, curving under her bottom, and his fingers dipped between her legs. She gasped, arching into him as an almost electric sensation sparked through her. One finger explored deeper, slipping a little way into her. A soft, wild noise erupted from her throat, and she all but climbed him, one leg wrapping around him as she levered herself up so he could have better access.

Panting, she buried her face in his throat, clinging for dear life while she waited in agony for him to deepen the caress. Slowly, so slowly, that big finger pressed deeper and she rocked under the impact. That wild little noise sounded again, and her hips surged, trying to take more of his finger. Pleasure and tension coiled in her, tighter and tighter, until it was pain and something more, something beyond anything she had imagined.

"Not yet," he said urgently. "Don't come yet." He turned and half-fell with her onto the bed, cradling her against the full impact of his weight as he landed on top of her. With a twist of his hips he settled between her thighs, and his erection prodded at her folds, briefly seeking her entrance before finding it and pressing inward. Her entire body contracted, tightening around that thick intrusion, though she couldn't tell whether her body's reaction was in welcome or an effort to limit the depth of his penetration.

His hips recoiled, his buttocks tightened, and he pushed deeper, deeper, until her inner resistance was gone and in one long slide he was all the way inside her.

She would have screamed, but her lungs were compressed with shock and she could barely breathe, much less scream. Her vision blurred and darkened. She hadn't realized. . . . His penis felt almost unbearably hot inside her, burning and stretching her. She ached deep inside, where he was.

He lifted up on his elbows, panting, the expres-

sion in his blue eyes both incredulous and fero-
ciously intent. "Lilah . . . God, I can't believe
this— Are you a virgin?"

"Not now." Desperately she clutched his buttocks, her back arching as she tried to take him
deeper. "Please. Oh, God, Jackson, please!" She
bucked her hips at him, her head thrown back as
she wrestled with the almost savage pleasure that
held her on the edge of release. He was still hurting her, but her entire body was throbbing with a
need that overrode any pain. She wanted him
deep, she wanted him hard, she wanted him to
pound into her and hurl her over that edge.

He gave in to her sensual imploring. "Shhh,"
he soothed, though his voice was rough with his
own need. "Easy, darlin'. Let me help . . ." He
reached between their bodies, his callused fingertips finding the bud of her clitoris and gently
pinching it up. Again and again he squeezed it,
catching it between two of his fingers, and with a
sharp cry she imploded, her body twisting and
heaving in the paroxysm of climax.

A harsh sound tore from his throat. He
gripped her hips, his fingers digging into her buttocks, and thrust hard, driving into her so fierce-

ly the bed thudded against the wall. He climaxed convulsively, grinding down on her for long seconds before collapsing, shaking, on top of her.

She wrapped her arms around his sweaty shoulders and held on tight, partly to comfort him in the aftermath and partly to anchor herself. She felt as if she would fly into a hundred pieces if she let him go. Tears burned her eyelids, though she didn't know why. Her heart still galloped in a mad race to nowhere and her thoughts swam, a kaleidoscope of impressions and wishes and disbelief.

She hadn't known making love would be so hot, so uncontrolled. She had expected something slow and sweet, building to ecstasy, not that headlong dash into the fire.

His heart pounded against her breast, gradually slowing, as did his breathing. His weight crushed her into the mattress. Her thighs were still spread to accommodate him, and he was still inside her, though smaller and softer now.

Now that the storm within was over, she became aware again of the storm without. Lightning cracked so close by that the thunder rattled the entire house, and rain drummed on the roof, but that was nothing compared to what had just gone on in her bed. Storms came and went, but her entire life had just been changed.

Finally he lifted his head. His dark hair was matted with sweat, his expression strained and empty, the expression of release. "Okay." His voice sounded rusty, as if his vocal cords didn't want to work. "When you said 'not now,' did you mean that you didn't want to talk, or that you had been a virgin until then, but now you weren't?"

She cleared her throat. "The second choice." Her own voice sounded rusty, too.

"Holy hell." He let his head drop again. "I never expected— Damn it, Lilah, that's something you should tell a man."

She moved her hands over his shoulders, closing her eyes in delight at the feel of his warm, sleek skin under her palms. "Things happened kind of fast. I didn't have a lot of time to consider the shoulds and should nots."

"There are no should nots, in this case."

"What would you have done differently, if you'd known?"

He considered that, and sighed against her shoulder. "Hell, probably nothing. There's no way in hell I would have stopped. But if I'd known, I'd have tried to slow things down, and given you more time."

"I couldn't have stood it," she said starkly. "Not one minute more."

"Yes you could. You will. And you'll like it."

If that was a threat, it failed miserably. A tingle of excitement shot through her, sending a spark of life into her exhausted muscles. She wiggled a little. "When?"

"God," he muttered. "Not right this minute. Give me an hour."

"Okay, an hour."

His head came up again and he gave her a long, level look. "Before we get carried away again, don't you think we need to talk about birth control? Specifically, our lack of it? I doubt you're on the pill, and I don't generally carry rubbers around with me."

"No, of course I'm not on the pill, but I won't get pregnant."

"You can't be sure."

"I just finished my period two days ago. We're safe."

"Famous last words."

She sighed. She *knew* she wouldn't get pregnant, though she didn't know how to explain to him how she knew. She wasn't certain, herself. It wasn't a flash of precognition, at least not like the usual flash. It was more a sense than a knowing, but there wasn't a pregnancy in her immediate future. Next month, maybe, but not now.

She sighed. "If you're so worried, then we won't do this again, all right?"

He regarded her for a minute, then grinned. "Some chances," he said, leaning down to kiss her, "are just meant to be taken."

7

They heard the outboard motor not long after dawn, when the sun had just turned the eastern sky a brilliant gold. The storms of the night had lasted longer than expected, until almost three o'clock in the morning, but now the morning sky was absolutely cloudless.

"Sounds like the cavalry is arriving," Lilah said, tilting her head to listen.

"Son of a bitch," Jackson said mildly. "I was hoping rescue would take a little longer." He took a sip of coffee. "Do I look like an enraged, frustrated sheriff who was left stranded by a turnip-brain two-bit thug, or a man who's had a night-long orgy and whose legs are as limp as noodles?"

She pretended to study him, then shook her head. "You could use some practice on the enraged and frustrated look."

"That's what I thought." Putting his cup down on the table, he stretched his arms over his head and gave her a lazy, contented grin. "Instead of arresting Thaniel, I may give him a commendation."

"What are you going to arrest him for?" she asked in surprise. "I told you I'm not pressing charges."

"Whether or not you do, he stole two boats, not just yours. What happens depends on what he's done with Jerry Watkins's boat, and what Jerry wants to do about it. If Thaniel was smart, he left the boats at the launch ramp, but then again, if he was smart he wouldn't have taken them in the first place."

"If he left them out, the amount of rain we had last night would have sunk them," Lilah pointed out. "It takes a lot of rain to swamp a boat, but I think we had enough to do the job, don't you?"

"Probably." Getting up from the table, he walked into the living room and looked out the window. "Yep, it's the cavalry."

Lilah stood beside him and watched the boat carrying two deputies approach her small dock. The river was high and muddy after the night's storms, so high her dock lacked only a few inches being underwater. They carefully tied the boat to the post and stepped out, both wearing Kevlar vests and carrying shotguns. They cautiously looked around.

Jackson quickly bent and kissed her, his mouth warm and lingering. The look he gave her was full of regret. "I'll come back as soon as I can," he said, keeping his voice pitched low. "I doubt it'll be today, and whether or not I can make it tomorrow depends on how much damage the storms did, and if there are any power outages or cleanup to do."

"I'll be here," she said, her manner calm. She smiled. "I have no way of going anywhere, without my boat."

"I'll either get it back, or I'll make damn certain Thaniel buys you a new one," he promised, and kissed her again. Then he picked up his vest and shotgun, which he had placed by the front door in anticipation of his "rescue," and walked out onto the front porch.

Both of the deputies visibly relaxed when they saw him. "You okay, Sheriff?" the older of the two called.

"I'm fine, Lowell. But Thaniel Vargas won't be when I get my hands on him. He stole both the boat I was using, and Miss Jones's boat. But he'll wait; how much damage was there last night?"

Lilah stepped out on the porch behind him, because it would look strange if she didn't. "Good morning, Lowell." She nodded to the other deputy. "Alvin. I just made the sheriff some coffee; would y'all like a cup?" She saw Jackson's brows rise in surprise that she knew his deputies, but he didn't comment.

"No thanks, Lilah," Lowell answered. "We need to get on back. Thanks for offering, but I've drunk so much coffee since midnight I doubt I'll sleep for two days."

"The damage?" Jackson prompted, taking charge of the conversation again.

"Power was out over most of the county, but it's back on now all except for Pine Flats. A lot of trees went down, and there's roof damage to a bunch of houses, but only one actually went into a house, the LeCroy place out near Washington

High School. Mrs. LeCroy was hurt pretty bad; she's in the hospital in Mobile."

"Any car wrecks?"

Lowell gave him a weary look. "More than you can count."

"Okay. Sorry I wasn't on hand to help."

"I'm just sorry it took us so long to get out here, but with the storms the way they were, only a fool would have gone out on the water."

"I didn't expect anybody to risk their lives coming after me. I was okay, just stranded."

"We weren't sure, what with Jo telling us she sent you here after Thaniel Vargas. But Thaniel seemed okay, not nervous or anything, and he played dumb, said he hadn't been up here and hadn't seen you."

"You saw him?" Jackson asked sharply.

"He helped us get a tree out of the highway. Anyway, we figured the storm had caught you. We didn't want to take any chances, since you could have run into some other kind of trouble out here, so we came looking."

Jackson shook his head. He never would have figured Thaniel capable of that much brass; maybe that thick-headed act was more of an act than fact. If so, he'd have to take Thaniel a lot more seriously than he had before. Walking down to the dock, he handed the shotgun to Alvin and stepped into the boat. "Well, let's go to work," he said. He turned and raised his hand. "Thanks for feeding me, Miss Jones."

"You're welcome," she called, smiling as she hugged her arms against the early-morning chill. She waved them good-bye, a wave both deputies returned, then went back into the house.

Jackson settled onto a boat seat. "Y'all seem to know Miss Jones pretty well," he said, driven by curiosity.

"Sure." Lowell got behind the wheel. "We went to school together."

It was such a prosaic answer that Jackson felt like smacking himself in the head. Of course she had attended school; she hadn't lived her entire life marooned upriver. He had a mental image of a small, solemn Lilah sitting in that little flat-bottom boat, clutching her schoolbooks, being ferried back and forth in all kinds of weather.

Because he wanted to know, he asked, "How did she get back and forth to school?"

"Boat," Alvin said. "Her daddy brought her.

He'd take her to the park ramp, closest to school. If the weather was good, he'd walk her the rest of the way. If it was raining, a teacher would meet them and give her a ride."

At least he wouldn't have to fret about that young Lilah being left alone at the boat docks, Jackson thought; her father had been concerned for her safety. Though why he would fret about something so long in the past was beyond him.

The trip downriver was much more leisurely than his risky dash up it the day before. The swollen river was full of trash, making caution necessary. Jackson hoped he'd see two boats tied to the shore when they got to the ramp, but no such luck.

"I wonder what Thaniel did with Jerry Watkins's boat," he growled.

"No telling," Lowell said. "The damn fool probably just turned it loose. Jerry will be fit to be tied; he set a store by that boat."

At least Jerry Watkins would have insurance on his boat; Jackson very much doubted Lilah would have it on hers. How would she replace it? He gave his bank account a quick mental check; one way or the other, Lilah would have another boat—

by tomorrow, if he couldn't find hers. He couldn't bear the thought of her being completely stranded out there, though she was so damn competent he could see her hiking into town if necessary, even though it had to be twenty, maybe thirty miles around. But what if she got sick, or injured herself. She chopped her own wood, for God's sake. He went cold at the thought of an ax buried in her foot.

She had become more important to him, faster than anyone he had ever known. Twenty-four hours ago he hadn't known she existed. Within two hours of meeting her, he'd been in bed with her, and he'd spent the most erotic, exciting night of his life in her arms. He had climaxed so many times he doubted he'd get a hard-on for days. Then he thought of Lilah, waiting for him, and a sudden pooling of heat in his groin told him he had miscalculated. He jerked his thoughts back to the day's work before he embarrassed himself.

The Watkins truck was still sitting where Charlotte had parked it, boat trailer still hitched to it. At least a tree hadn't come down on the truck during the storms; that would be the final insult to a good deed. He looked around; there were some small branches scattered around the parking area, but nothing substantial.

Lowell eased the boat into the bank and both Jackson and Alvin climbed out. While Alvin went to the truck to back the trailer into the water, Jackson surveyed the area. Yesterday he'd been in too much of a hurry to think about details, but now his cop's eye swept the launch ramp, not missing a thing. The parking area was surprisingly large, given how isolated and little-used the launch ramp was. But . . . was it little-used? The area was free of weeds, showing that there was a good bit of traffic. The sandy dirt showed evidence of a lot of different tire tracks, more than he expected. That was strange, given what Jo had said about the best fishing being downriver.

Lowell and Alvin competently took the boat out of the water. They had come in two vehicles, one county car and then the truck pulling the boat, which Jackson assumed they had borrowed from the Rescue Squad. That made five vehicles he could count since yesterday afternoon: his, Thaniel's, Charlotte Watkins's, and now these two. The rain had destroyed all but the deepest tracks, but he could still make out at least three more sets of tracks besides the ones he knew about.

Now, why would there be so much river traffic up here? The fishing wasn't good, and right past Lilah's the river got too shallow for boat traffic. He tried to think of a logical explanation for the tracks. Being in law enforcement, his first thought was that maybe drug dealers were meeting here, but he discarded that idea. It was too open, and though Old Boggy Road wasn't the busiest road in the world, there was occasional traffic on it. As if to prove it, at that moment a farmer drove by in a pickup truck, and he craned his neck to see what was going on.

No, drug dealers would find a place where they were less likely to attract attention. So . . . who was coming here, and why?

He strolled over to Lowell and Alvin. "This little ramp gets a lot of use, doesn't it?"

"A fair amount," Lowell agreed.

"Why?"

They both gaped at him. "Why?" Alvin echoed.

"Yeah. Why does it get so much use? Only

someone who doesn't know the river would come up here to fish."

To his surprise, both deputies shifted uncomfortably. Lowell cleared his throat. "I guess folks go to visit Lilah."

"Miss Jones?" Jackson clarified, wanting to make certain there wasn't another Lilah in the area.

Lowell nodded.

Looking around the area, Jackson said, "From all these tire ruts, I'd say she gets a lot of company." He tried to picture a steady stream of visitors to Lilah's isolated little house upriver, but just couldn't.

"Some," Lowell agreed. "A lot of women go to see her." He coughed. "And—uh, some men, too, I guess."

"Why is that?" A variety of wild reasons ran through his mind. Marijuana? He couldn't see Lilah growing marijuana, but the place was certainly isolated enough. He didn't let himself seriously consider that. Women didn't go to backwoods women for abortions anymore, either, so that was out. Nothing illegal, for sure, because his deputies obviously knew about whatever was going on up there, and had done nothing to stop it. The only thing he could think of that made sense was so ridiculous he couldn't believe it.

"Don't tell me she really is a witch!" He could just see it now, boat after boat making its way upriver for spells and potions. She had denied the witch thing, said she didn't know anything about spells, but in his experience people lied all the time. He dealt with serial liars on a daily basis.

"Nothing like that," Alvin said hastily. "She's kind of an old-timey healer. You know, she makes poultices and stuff."

Poultices and stuff. Healer. Of course. It was so obvious, Jackson wondered that he hadn't seen it. Relief spread through him. His imagination had been running wild, a sick feeling congealing in his gut. He had just found her, a woman who appealed to him on every level, and he couldn't bear the thought of her being involved in something shifty. He didn't know where this thing between him and Lilah was going, but he intended to follow it to the end.

"It's how she makes her living," Lowell said. "People buy herbs and things from her. A lot of folks go to her rather than a doctor, because she's so good at telling them what's wrong."

He wanted to grin. Instead he collected his vest and shotgun from the boat and said, "Well, let's go round up Thaniel Vargas. Even if we get the boats back and Jerry Watkins doesn't press charges against him, I want to scare about ten years off the bastard's life."

8

Thaniel Vargas was nowhere to be found. He had gone to ground somewhere, Jackson figured, waiting for the trouble to blow over. Because things were still kind of busy in the county, with the continuing power outage in Pine Flats and cleaning up from the storm, Jackson couldn't devote a lot of time or manpower to finding him.

More than anything, he wanted to get back upriver to Lilah's house, but it just wasn't possible that day. Besides the problems from the storm, the blue moon craziness was still in full force. At traffic court that day, a woman totally lost it and tried to get out of paying a speeding ticket by holding the judge hostage. Why anyone in her right mind would want to trade a simple fine of fifty bucks for a felony charge was beyond Jackson. Getting the courthouse settled down took several hours out of his day, hours when he needed to be somewhere else.

He got home at midnight that night, tired and disgruntled and aching with frustration. He wanted Lilah. He *needed* Lilah, needed the simple serenity of her, the quietness of her home that was such a contrast to his hectic days. They had known each other for such a short period of time, he wasn't certain that they had anything more than a one-night stand, brought about as much by circumstance as by mutual attraction. But he had been her first lover, her only lover; Lilah wasn't the type of woman to have a one-night stand. For her, making love meant something. It had meant something to him, too, something more than any of his other love affairs.

Lilah was special: honest, witty, with the bite of irony he enjoyed, and gutsy. She was also sexy as hell, with her well-toned, femininely muscled body and her cloud of curly hair that just begged to have his hands in it.

Though he was her first lover, she hadn't shrunk from anything he wanted to do. She had met him halfway in everything, enjoying what he did to her as much as he enjoyed doing it, and returning the favor. He couldn't imagine such uncomplicated joy ever getting boring.

Until now, his house had suited him perfectly. It was an older house, with high ceilings and cranky plumbing, but he'd had the main bathroom completely redone, and the kitchen, not that he was much on cooking. It had just seemed like a smart thing to do. His bed was big enough for him, not like Lilah's too-short, too-narrow bed. They'd had to sleep double-decker, when they slept—not a big sacrifice. He'd liked having her sprawled on top of him, when he wasn't on top of her.

But now his house felt . . . empty. And noisy. He hadn't realized until now how much noise a refrigerator made, or a water heater. The central air system blotted out the night's sounds of crickets and the occasional chirp of a bird.

He wanted Lilah.

He took a cold shower instead, and crawled into his big, cold, empty bed, where he lay awake, muscles aching, eyes burning with fatigue, and thought of that first searing, electric moment when he pushed into Lilah's body. That got him so hard he groaned, and he tried not to think about sex at all. But then her breasts came to mind, and he remembered the way her nipples had peaked in his mouth when he sucked her, and how she had moaned and squirmed when he went down on her.

Sweat sheened his body, despite the air conditioning. Swearing, he got out of bed and took another cold shower. He finally got to sleep about two o'clock, only to dream erotic dreams and wake up needing, wanting Lilah even more than before.

AT EIGHT TWENTY-ONE in the morning, Thaniel Vargas's body was found floating in the river. He was easily identified because his wallet was still stuffed in his jeans pocket, along with a can of chewing tobacco. If it hadn't been for his wallet, his own mother would have been hard-pressed to identify him, because he'd been shot in the face with a shotgun.

"I don't think he's been dead long," the coroner said, standing beside Jackson as the body was wrapped and loaded in a meat wagon. "The turtles and fish hadn't been at him much. As fast as the river's flowing, the current would have kept him on the surface, plus that dead branch his arm was tangled in gave him added buoyancy."

"How long?"

"It's just a guess, Jackson. I'd say . . . twelve hours or so. Hard to tell, when they've been in the water. But he was last seen night before last, so it couldn't have been much longer than half a day."

Jackson stared at the river, a sick feeling shredding his guts into confetti as he thought this through. He plainly remembered Lilah staring at Thaniel and saying, "You're dead," in that flat, unemotional tone that had been even more chilling than if she had screamed it at him. And now Thaniel *was* dead, from a shotgun blast. Lilah had a shotgun. Had Thaniel gone back to her house yesterday, or even last night? Had she made good on her threat, if it had indeed been one?

That was the best-case scenario, that Lilah had been forced to defend herself, or even that she had shot Thaniel at first sight. He didn't like it, but he could understand if a woman alone shot first and asked questions later when a thug who had been shooting at her the day before came back for more target practice. He doubted the district attorney would even indict under those circumstances.

Worst-case scenario, however, was the possibility that Lilah was lying in a pool of blood at her house, wounded or even dead. The thought galvanized him, sending pure panic racing through his bloodstream.

"Hal, I need that boat!" he roared at the captain of the Rescue Squad, referring to the boat they had used to retrieve Thaniel's body from the river. He was already striding toward the boat as he yelled.

Hal looked up, his homely face showing only mild surprise. "Okay, Sheriff," he said. "Anything I can help you with?"

"I'm going up to Lilah Jones's place. If Thaniel went back to shoot up the place again, she might be hurt." *Or dead.* But he didn't let himself dwell on that. He couldn't, and still function.

"If she's hurt, she'll need medical attention, and transport. I'll call for another boat and follow you." Hal unclipped the radio from his belt and rapped out instructions.

The Rescue Squad boats were built for stability, not speed, which was a good thing in the roiling river, with all the broken limbs and debris floating downstream, but Jackson still cursed the lack of speed. He needed to get to Lilah. Desperation gnawed at him, tearing at him with the knowledge that, if she had been shot, if she still lived, every second help was delayed could mean she wouldn't survive. He knew gunshot wounds; damn few of them were immediately fatal. A head or heart shot were about the only ones that could kill on contact, and that wasn't guaranteed.

He couldn't think of her lying bleeding and helpless, her life slowly ebbing away. He couldn't. And yet he couldn't stop, because his experience gave him graphic knowledge. Images rolled through his mind, an endless tape that made him sicker and sicker.

"Please. God, *please.*" He heard himself praying aloud, saying the words into the wind.

Getting to Lilah's house took forever. He had started out much farther down the river than from the ramp on Old Boggy Road. He had to dodge debris, and a couple of times the boat shuddered over submerged limbs. The engine stalled the last time, but it restarted on the first try. If it hadn't, he probably would have jumped into the river and swam the rest of the way.

At last the house came into view, nestled under the trees. Heart pounding, he searched for any sign of life, but the morning was still and quiet. Surely Lilah would have come out on the porch when she heard the outboard motor, if she was there. But where else could she be? She had no means of transportation.

"Lilah!" he yelled. "Lilah!" She had to be there, but he found himself hoping she wasn't, hoping she had gone for a walk in the woods, or borrowed a boat from some of the multitude who evidently found their way to her house for folk remedies. He hoped—God, he hoped almost anything at all had taken her away from the house, rather than think she didn't come out on the porch because she was lying somewhere dead or dying.

He nosed the boat up to the dock and tied it to the post. *"Lilah!"*

Boots thudding, he raced up the dock just as he had two days before, but the adrenaline burn he'd felt then was nothing compared to the inferno he felt now, as if he might burst out of his skin.

He leaped onto the porch, bypassing the steps. The windows on this side of the house were intact, he noted. He wrenched open the screen door and turned the knob of the main door; it was unlocked, and swung inward.

He stepped into the cool, dim house, his head thrown up as he sniffed the air. The house smelled as before: fragrant and welcoming, the faint odor of biscuits lingering, probably from last night's supper. The windows were up and pristine white curtains fluttered in the slight morning breeze. No odor of death hung like a miasma, nor could he detect the flat, metallic smell of blood.

She wasn't in the house. He went through it anyway, checking all four rooms. The house seemed undisturbed.

He went outside, circling the house, looking for any signs of violence. Nothing. Chickens clucked contentedly, pecking at bugs. Birds sang. Eleanor waddled out from under the porch, still fat with kittens. He stooped to pet her, his head swiveling as he checked every detail of his surroundings. "Where is she, Eleanor?" he whispered. Eleanor purred, and rubbed her head against his hand.

"Lilah!" he roared. Eleanor started, and retreated under the porch again.

"I'm coming."

The voice was faint, and came from behind the house. He jerked around, staring into the trees. The woods were almost impenetrable; he could be right on her, and not be able to see her.

"Where are you?" he called, striding rapidly to the back of the house.

"Almost there." Two seconds later she emerged from the trees, carrying a basket—and the shotgun. "I heard the outboard," she said as he reached her, "but I was a couple of hundred yards away and—uumph."

The rest of her words were lost under the fierce assault of his mouth. He hauled her up against him, unable to hold her close enough. He wanted to meld her into his very flesh, and never let her go. She was okay. She was alive, unharmed, warm and vibrant in his arms. The wind blew her soft curls around his face. He drank in her smell, fresh and soft, womanly. She tasted the same, her mouth answering his. He heard the basket drop to the ground, and the shotgun, then her arms were around him and she was clinging tightly to him.

Need roared through him like an inferno, born of his desperate fear and relief. He tore at her clothes, stripping down her jeans and panties and lifting her out of them.

"Jackson?" Her head lolled back, her breath coming in soft pants. "Let's go inside——"

"I can't wait," he muttered savagely, lifting her up and backing her against a tree. Her legs came up and locked around his hips as she automatically sought to balance herself. He wrenched his pants open, freed himself, and shoved into her. She was hot and damp and tight, her inner flesh enveloping and clasping. She wasn't ready for him; he heard her gasp, but he couldn't stop. He pulled back and thrust again and he went all the way in this time. On the fifth thrust he began coming, his body heaving against her as he spurted for what seemed like forever, until his head swam and his vision blurred and darkened, and still the spasms took a long time to die down, small bursts of sensation rocking him. He sank heavily against her, pinning her to the tree. His legs trembled, and his lungs heaved. "I love you," he heard himself muttering. "Oh, God, I was so scared."

Her hands were clasping his head, stroking,

trying to soothe him. "Jackson? What's wrong? What happened?"

He couldn't speak for a minute, still in shock from what he had said. The words had just boiled out, without thought. He hadn't said those words to any woman since his high school days, when he fell in love on a regular basis.

But they were true, he realized, and that shocked him almost as much as saying them. He loved her. He, Jackson Brody, was *in love*. It had happened too fast for him to come to terms with it, to think about it as they gradually became enmeshed in each other's lives. Logic said he couldn't possibly love her after so short a time; emotion said to hell with logic, he loved her.

"Jackson?"

He tried to pull away from that emotional brink, to function as a sheriff instead of a man. He had come here because a man had been murdered, and somewhere along the line he had forgotten that and focused, instead, on the woman at the center of the situation. But he was still inside her, still dazed from the force of his orgasm, and all he could do was sink more heavily against her, pressing her into the tree trunk. Birds sang around him, insects buzzed, the river murmured. Bright morning sunlight worked its way through the thick canopy of leaves, dappling their skin.

"I'm sorry," he managed to say. "Did I hurt you?" He knew he had entered her far too roughly, and she hadn't been aroused and ready.

"Some." She sounded remarkably peaceful. "At first. Then I enjoyed it."

He snorted. "You couldn't have enjoyed it very much. I think I lasted about five seconds." The sheriff still hadn't made an appearance; the man held full sway.

"I enjoyed *your* pleasure." She kissed his neck. "It was actually rather . . . thrilling."

"I was scared to death," he admitted baldly.

"Scared? About what?"

Finally, belatedly, the sheriff lifted his head. Jackson discovered he couldn't question her, or even talk about Thaniel, while in his present position. Gently he withdrew from her and eased his weight back, holding her steady while her legs slipped from around his hips and she was once more standing on her own two feet.

"We'd better hurry," he said, picking up her clothes and handing them to her, then pulling up his own pants and getting everything tucked back in place. "The Rescue Squad could be here any minute."

"Rescue Squad?" she echoed, brows lifting in surprise.

He waited until she was dressed. "I was afraid you'd been hurt."

"Why would I be hurt?" She still looked totally bewildered.

As a man, he hated having to question her. As a sheriff, he knew he had to do it or resign today. "Thaniel Vargas's body was found this morning."

A stillness came over her, and she looked at him but somehow she wasn't seeing him, her gaze turned inward. "I knew he'd die," she finally said.

"He didn't *die*," Jackson corrected. "He was murdered. Shot in the face with a shotgun."

She came back from wherever she had gone, and her green eyes focused sharply on him. "You think I did it," she said.

9

I was afraid he'd come back and y'all started shooting at each other again. I was afraid I'd find you dead, or dying." His voice was remarkably calm, considering how shaken he felt.

She shook her head. "I haven't seen Thaniel since day before yesterday, but I don't have any way to prove it."

"Lilah." He gripped her shoulders, shaking her a little to get her attention. "You seem to think I'm going to take you in for murder. Baby, even if you did kill him, after what happened no D.A. would prosecute, at least not the D.A. here. But I don't think you could murder anyone, not even

Thaniel, and he was one worthless jackass. If you say you didn't kill him, then I believe you." The man was speaking again. The sheriff struggled to regain his detachment, though he thought it was a losing cause. He would never be detached when it came to Lilah.

She stared at him, a sense of wonderment coming to her eyes. In a flash of intuition he knew then she hadn't believed him when he blurted out that he loved her. Why should she? Men said "I love you" all the time in the heat of passion. And they had known each other less than two days. He was acutely aware that she hadn't said anything about love in return, but that would wait.

"But one thing keeps eating at me. Day before yesterday, you looked at him and said, 'You're dead,' and damn near scared him to death right then." He didn't ask anything, didn't try to form her answer in any way. He wanted her response to come from her own thoughts.

To his surprise, she went pale. She looked away, staring at the river. "I just—knew," she finally said, her voice stifled.

"Knew?"

"Jackson, I—" She half-turned away from him,

then turned back. She lifted her hands in a help-less gesture. "I don't know how to explain it."

"In English. That's my only requirement."

"I just know things. I get flashes."

"Flashes?"

Again the helpless gesture. "It isn't a vision, not exactly. I don't really *see* anything, I just *know*. Like intuition, only more."

"So you had one of these flashes about Thaniel?"

She nodded. "I looked at him when I came out on the porch and all of a sudden I knew he was going to die. I didn't know he was going to get killed. Just . . . that he wasn't going to be here any-more."

He rubbed the back of his neck. In the distance he could hear the droning of an outboard motor: the Rescue Squad was getting close.

"I've never been wrong," she said, almost apol-ogetically.

"No one else knows what you said." His voice was as somber as he felt. "Just me."

She bent her head, and he saw her worrying her lower lip. She saw his dilemma. Then she raised her head and squared her shoulders. "You

233

have to do your job. You can't keep this to yourself, and be a good sheriff."

If he hadn't already known he loved her, that moment would have done it for him. And suddenly he knew something else. "Are these 'flashes' the reason Thaniel thought you're a witch?"

She gave him a rueful little smile. "I wasn't very good at hiding things when I was young. I blabbed."

"Scared him, huh? And all these people who come to you for treatment—you just look at them and have flashes about what's wrong with them?"

"Of course not," she said, startled. Then she blushed. "That's something else."

The blush both intrigued and alarmed him. "What kind of something else?"

"You'll think I'm a freak," she said in dismay.

"But a sexy freak. Tell me." A little bit of the sheriff was in his tone, a quiet authority.

"I see auras. You know, the colors that everyone has around them. I know what the different colors mean, and if someone's sick I can see where and know what to do, whether or not I can help them or they need to see a doctor."

Auras. Jackson wanted to sit down. He'd heard

all that New Age mumbo-jumbo, but that's just what it was, as far as he was concerned. He'd never seen a nimbus of color around anyone, never seen proof such a thing existed.

"I haven't told anyone about the auras," she said, her voice shaking. "They just think I'm a . . . a medicine woman, like my mother. She saw them, too. I remember her telling me, when I was little, what the different colors meant. That's how I learned my colors." She gave a quick look at the river, where the boat had come into view. Tears welled in her eyes. "You have the most beautiful aura," she whispered. "So clean and rich and healthy. I knew as soon as I saw you that—"

She broke off, and he didn't pursue it. The Rescue Squad boat had reached her dock, and the two men in it were getting out. One was Hal, who had come along himself to take charge if the Squad was needed, and the other was a tall, thin man Jackson recognized as a medic, though he didn't know his name.

Lilah did, though. She left Jackson's side and walked out of the trees into the open, her hand lifted in a wave.

Both men waved back. "Glad to see you're

okay," Hal called as they started up the dock.

"Just fine, thanks. Thaniel hadn't been here, though."

"Yeah, we know." Hal looked past Lilah to Jackson. "You left about a minute too soon, Sheriff. I still can't believe it."

"Believe what?"

"Jerry Watkins drove up just as you went out of sight. We were just getting the boat in the water. I tell you, Jerry looked like hell, like he'd been on a weeklong bender. He looked at the body bag in the meat wagon and just broke down, crying like a baby. He's the one killed Thaniel, Sheriff. He jumped Thaniel about his boat, and you know how Thaniel was, too stupid to know when to back down. He told Jerry he sunk the son of a bitch. Beg pardon, Lilah. Jerry set a store by that boat. The way he tells it, he lost all control, grabbed the shotgun from his truck, and let Thaniel have it."

After years in law enforcement, little could surprise Jackson. He wasn't surprised now, because dumber things had happened. And though the full moon was waning, weird things would continue to happen for another couple of days. He did feel as if he'd dropped the ball, however. He should have thought of Jerry. Everyone who knew Jerry knew how he loved that boat. Instead he'd been so focused on Lilah that he hadn't been able to see anything else.

"He sat down on the ground and put his hands on his head for your deputies to arrest him. Guess he saw that on television," Hal finished.

Well, that was that. Thaniel's murder was solved before it had time to become a real mystery. But one little detail struck him as strange. Jackson looked at the medic. "If you knew Lilah was okay, that Thaniel hadn't been killed in a fight here, why did you come along?"

"He came to see me," Lilah said. She shook her head. "I can't help you, Cory. You've got gallstones. You're going to have to see a doctor."

"Ah, hell, Lilah, I haven't even told you my symptoms!"

"You don't have to tell me, I can see how you look. It hurts like blue blazes every time you eat, doesn't it? Were you afraid you were having heart problems, maybe?"

Cory made a face. "How'd you know?"

"Just a hunch. Go see that doctor. There's a

237

good gastro specialist in Montgomery. I'll give you his name."

"Okay," he said glumly. "I was hoping it was an ulcer and you could give me something for it."

"Nope. Surgery."

"Damn."

"Well, that's taken care of," Hal said. "We'd better get back, we still got some more work to do in Pine Flats. Will you be along soon, Jackson?"

"In a little while," Jackson said. From the way Hal winked, he figured the older man had cottoned on to the fact that there was something between him and Lilah. Frankly, Jackson didn't care if the whole county knew.

He and Lilah watched the two men get back into the boat and head back downriver. Jackson squinted his eyes in the bright sun. "Auras, huh?" What the hell. If he believed she could have flashes of precognition, why not auras? If you loved someone, he thought, you accepted a lot of stuff that you never would have considered before. Privately, he'd check on Cory's diagnosis from a doctor, just to make sure, but for some reason he figured Lilah had been right. Auras were as good a reason as anything.

She reached for his hand. "I told you that you have a beautiful aura. I probably would have loved you just because of what I saw in it. But I had another flash when I saw you the first time."

He closed his hand warmly around hers. "What did that one tell you?"

She gave him a somber look. "That you were going to be the love of my life."

He felt a little light-headed. Maybe it was just the culmination of a very stressful morning, but he remembered that feeling of dizziness the first time he'd seen *her.* "Didn't you say those flashes had never been wrong?"

"That's right." She rose on tiptoe and kissed him. "They're one-hundred-percent accurate."

He needed to get back to work. He needed to do a lot of things. But he didn't need to do them as much as he needed to hold her, so he wrapped his arms around her and held her tight, breathing in the essence of the love of *his* life, so happy he thought he might burst.

"We're going to do this up right," he said aloud. "The whole enchilada. Marriage. Kids."

"The whole enchilada," she agreed, and hand in hand they walked into the house.

WHITE OUT

1

I t was going to snow.

The sky was low and flat, an ominous purplish gray that blended into and obscured the mountaintops, so that it was difficult to tell where the earth stopped and the sky began. The air had a sharp, ammonia smell to it, and the icy edge of the wind cut through Hope Bradshaw's jeans as if they were made of gauze instead of thick denim. The trees moaned under the lash of the wind, branches rustling and whipping, the low, mournful sound settling in her bones.

She was too busy to stand around staring at the clouds, but she was nevertheless always aware of them hovering, pressing closer. A sense of urgency kept her moving, checking the generator and making sure she had plenty of fuel handy for it, carrying extra wood into her çabin and stacking even more on the broad, covered porch behind the kitchen. Maybe her instincts were wrong and the snow wouldn't amount to any more than the four to six inches the weather forecasters were predicting.

She trusted her instincts, though. This was her seventh winter in Idaho, and every time there had been a big snow, she had gotten this same crawly feeling just before it. The atmosphere was charged with energy, Mother Nature gathering herself for a real blast. Whether caused by static electricity or plain old foreboding, her spine was tingling from an uneasiness that wouldn't let her rest.

She wasn't worried about surviving: she had food, water, shelter. This was, however, the first time Hope had gone through a big snow alone. Dylan had been here the first two years; after he died, her dad had moved to Idaho to help her take care of the resort. But her uncle Pete had suffered a heart attack three days ago, and her dad had flown to Indianapolis to be with his oldest brother. Uncle Pete's prognosis was good: the heart attack was relatively mild, and he had gotten to the hospital soon enough to minimize the damage. Her dad planned to stay another week, since he hadn't seen any of his brothers or sisters in over a year.

She didn't *mind* being alone, but securing the cabins was a lot of work for one person. There were eight of them, single-storied, some with one bedroom and some with two, sheltered by towering trees. There were four on one side of her own, much larger A-frame cabin, and four on the other side, the nine buildings curving around the bank of a picturesque lake that was teeming with fish. She had to make certain the doors and windows were securely fastened against what could be a violent wind, and water valves had to be turned off and pipes drained so they wouldn't freeze and burst when the power went off, which she had absolute faith would happen. Losing power wasn't a matter of *if*, but *when*.

Actually, the weather had been mild this year; though it was December, there had been only one snow, a measly few inches, the remnants of which still lingered in the shaded areas and crunched under her boots. The ski resorts were hurting; their owners would welcome even a blizzard, if it left behind a good, thick base.

Even the infamously optimistic slobber-hound, a golden retriever otherwise known as Tinkerbell even though he was neither female nor a fairy, seemed to be worrying about the weather. He stayed right behind her as she trudged from cabin to cabin, sitting on the porch while she worked inside, his tail thumping on the planks in relieved greeting when she reappeared. "Go chase a rabbit or something," she told him after she almost stumbled over him as she left the next to last cabin, but though his brown eyes lit with enthusiasm at the idea, he declined the invitation.

Those brown eyes were irresistible, staring up at her with love and boundless trust. Hope squatted down and rubbed behind his ears, sending him into twisting, whining ecstasy as he all but collapsed under the pleasure. "You big mutt," she said lovingly, and he responded to the tone with a swipe of his tongue on her hand.

Tink was five; she had gotten him the month after Dylan died, before her dad had come to live with her. The clumsy, adorable, loving ball of fuzz seemed to sense her sadness and had devoted himself to making her laugh with his antics. He smothered her with affection, licking whatever part of her was within reach, crying at night until she surrendered and lifted the puppy onto the bed with her, where he happily settled down against her, and the warmth of the little body in the night somehow made the loneliness more bearable.

Gradually the pain became less acute, her father arrived, and she was less lonely, and as he grew, Tink gradually distanced himself, moving from her bed to the rug beside it, then to the doorway, and finally down to the living room, as if he were weaning her from *his* presence. His accustomed sleeping spot now was on the rug in front of the fireplace, though he made periodic tours of the house during the night to make certain everything in his doggy world was okay.

Hope looked at Tink, and her lungs suddenly constricted, compressing as an enormous sense of panic seized her. He was five. Dylan had been dead *five* years! The impossibility of it stunned her, rocked her back. Hope stared, unseeing, at the dog, her eyes wide and fixed, her hand still on his head.

Five years. She was thirty-one, a widow who lived with her father and her dog, who hadn't been on a date in . . . God, almost two years now, and there had been a grand total of only three dates anyway. There weren't any neighbors nearby, the motel kept her busy during the summer when travel was easier, and she made it a point not to get involved with any of the guests, not that she had met any with whom she *wanted* to get involved.

Stricken, she looked around as if she didn't recognize her surroundings. There had been moments before when the reality of Dylan's death hit hard, but this was different. This was like being kicked in the chest.

Five years. Thirty-one. The numbers kept echoing in her mind, chasing each other in circles like maddened squirrels. What was she *doing* here? She was living her life secluded in the mountains, so immersed in being Dylan Bradshaw's widow that she had forgotten to be herself, running the small, exclusive resort that had been Dylan's dream.

Dylan's dream, not hers.

It had never been hers. Oh, she had been happy enough to come to Idaho with him, help him build his dream in the wilderness paradise, but her dream had been much simpler: a good marriage, kids, the kind of life her parents had enjoyed, piercingly sweet in its normalcy.

But Dylan was gone, his dream forever unfulfilled, and now hers was in danger too. She hadn't remarried, she had no children, and she was thirty-one.

"Oh, Tink," she whispered. For the first time she realized she might never remarry, might never have a family of her own. Where had the time gone? How had it slipped away, unnoticed?

As always, Tinkerbell sensed her mood and thrust himself closer to her, licking her hands, her cheek, her ear, almost knocking her down in his frenzy of sympathy. Hope grabbed him and regained her balance, laughing a little in spite of herself as she wiped away the slobber-hound's latest offering. "All right, all right, no more feeling sorry for myself. If I don't like what I've been doing, then change, right?"

His plumy tail wagged, his tongue lolled, and he grinned his doggy grin that said he approved of her speed in figuring out what she should do.

"Of course," she told him as she headed down

the trail toward the last cabin, "I have others to consider. I can't forget Dad. After all, he sold his house and came out here because of me. It wouldn't be fair to uproot him again, to say, 'Thanks for the support, but now it's time to move on.' And what about you, goofball? You're used to having plenty of room to roam, and let's face it, you aren't dainty."

Tink trotted after her, gamboling at her heels like an overgrown puppy, his ears pricked up as he listened to her tone. It was conversational, no longer sad, so his tail happily swished back and forth.

"Maybe I should just make an effort to get out more. The fact that I've only had three dates in five years *could* be my fault," Hope allowed wryly. "Let's face it, the drawback to living in a remote area is that there aren't many people around. *Duhh.*"

Tink stopped dead, bright eyes fastening on a squirrel scampering across the path in front of them. Without even an apologetic look for abandoning her, he tore out in furious pursuit of the squirrel, barking madly. Clearing Idaho of the villainous squirrels was Tink's ambition in life; though he had never caught one, he never stopped trying. After fruitlessly trying to break him of the habit, fearing he would tangle with a rabid squirrel, Hope had given up the effort and instead made certain he always got his rabies vaccination.

The squirrel scrambled up the nearest tree and stopped just out of reach of Tink's lunges, chattering at him and spurring Tink to even more barking and jumping, as if he suspected the varmint was mocking him.

Leaving the dog to his fun, Hope went up the steps to the long front porch of the last cabin. Though the little resort had been Dylan's idea, his dream, going into one of the cabins always gave her a sense of pride. He had designed them, but she was the one who had decorated them, took care of them. The furnishings were different in each one, but similar in their simplicity and comfort. The walls were decorated with tasteful prints, rather than ratty deer heads bought at garage sales. The furniture was comfortable enough for a couple on a honeymoon and substantial enough for a hunting party.

She had tried to make each one feel like a home instead of a rented cabin, with rugs and lamps and books, as well as a fully equipped kitchen. There were radios but no televisions, because reception in the mountains was so spotty and most of the guests mentioned how peaceful their stay was without it. There was a television in Hope's cabin, but it pulled in only one station during good weather and none at all during bad. She was considering investing in a satellite dish, because the winters were terribly long and often boring, and she and her dad could play only so many games of checkers.

If she did, she thought, she might add an extra receiver or two so a couple of the cabins could have television service to offer as an option. Things couldn't stay the same; if she kept the resort, she would have to continually make changes and improvements.

Taking a wrench from her hip pocket, she turned the valve that shut off the water to the cabin, then set about draining the pipes. The cabins were heated electrically, so when the power went off, they would quickly become icy inside. Each cabin did have a fireplace, but if a blizzard came, she certainly wouldn't be able to battle her way from cabin to cabin, building fires and keeping them fed.

That accomplished, she secured the shutters over the windows and locked the door. Tink had given up on the squirrel and was waiting for her on the porch. "That's it," she told him. "All finished. Just in time too," she added, as a snowflake drifted past her nose. "C'mon, let's go home."

He understood the word "home" and leaped to his feet, panting eagerly. A snowflake drifted past *his* nose, and he snapped at it, then was off on another manic tear, running back and forth, jumping at snowflakes and trying to catch them. His expression invited Hope to laugh at him, and she did, then joined him in a snowflake chase that turned into a game of tag, and ended with her running and jumping through the falling snow like a five-year-old herself. By the time she reached the big cabin, she was exhausted, panting harder than Tink and giggling at his antics.

He reached the door before she did, of course, and as always he was impatient to get inside. He turned his head to bark at her, demanding she hurry and open the door. "You're worse than having a child," she said, leaning over him to turn the doorknob. "You can't wait to get out, and once you're out, you can't wait to get back in. You'd better enjoy the outdoors while you can, because if this snow gets as bad as I think it will, it'll be a couple of days before you can go for a run."

Logic made no impression on Tink. He merely wagged his tail harder, and when the door opened, he lunged through the widening crack, yipping a little as he trotted around the spacious, two-story great room, checking all the familiar scents before darting into the kitchen and out again, then coming over to Hope as if to say, "I've checked things out and everything's okay." She patted him, then shed her heavy shearling coat and hung it on the hall tree, sighing in relief at the immediate sense of freedom and coolness.

Her home was beautiful, she thought, looking around. Not grand, not luxurious, but definitely beautiful. The front of the A-frame was a wall of windows, giving a wonderful view of the lake and the mountains. A big rock fireplace soared the entire two stories, and twin ceiling fans hung from the exposed-beam ceiling, circulating the warm air that gathered at the top back to the ground floor. Hope had a green thumb, and luxurious ferns and other houseplants gave the interior of the house a lush freshness. The floor was wide wood planking, finished to a pale gold and covered with thick area rugs in rich shades of blue and green. Graceful curving stairs wound up to the second floor, and the white stair railing continued across the balcony. For Christmas she always wound lights and greenery up the stair banisters and across the balcony, and the effect was breathtaking.

There were two bedrooms upstairs—the master bed and bath and a smaller bedroom, which they had intended to use for a nursery—and a large bedroom downstairs off the kitchen. Her dad used the downstairs bedroom, saying the stairs were hard on his knees, but the truth was the arrangement gave them both more privacy. The kitchen was spacious and efficient, with more cabinet space than she would ever use, a cook island she loved, and an enormous side-by-side refrigerator-freezer that could hold enough food to feed an army. There was also a well-stocked pantry, a small laundry room, and a powder room, and after her dad had moved in, Hope had added a small full bath to connect to his bedroom.

The total effect was undeniably beautiful and comfortable, but every time the electricity went off, Hope wished they had made better decisions about what would or would not be hard-wired to the generator. The refrigerator, cooktop, and water heater were connected. To save money by buying a smaller generator, they had decided not to connect the heating unit, the lights, or any wall plugs except those in the kitchen. In a power outage, they had reasoned, the fireplace in the great room would provide enough heat. Unfortunately, without the ceiling fans working to keep the air circulated, most of the heat produced by the fireplace went straight to the second floor. The upstairs would be stifling hot, while the downstairs remained chilly. The situation was livable, but not comfortable, especially for any length of time.

Forget the satellite dish, she thought. The money would be better spent on a larger generator and some electrical rewiring.

She looked out the windows; though it was only three o'clock, the clouds were so heavy it looked like twilight outside. The snow was falling faster now, fat, heavy flakes that had already dusted the ground with white just in the short time she had been inside.

She shivered suddenly, though the house was perfectly comfortable. A big pot of beef stew would hit the spot, she thought. And if the electricity was off for a long time, well, she might get awfully tired of beef stew, but reheating a bowl of it in the microwave drained a lot less power from the generator than cooking a small meal from scratch each time she got hungry.

But maybe she was wrong. Maybe it wouldn't snow that much.

2

She wasn't wrong.

The wind began howling, sweeping down from the icy mountaintops, and the snowfall grew steadily heavier. With nightfall, Hope could no longer see out the windows, so she opened the front door to peek out, and the savage wind slammed the door into her, almost knocking her down. Snow all but exploded into the great room. She couldn't see anything out there but a wall of white.

Panting, she grabbed the door and braced all her weight against it, forcing it shut. The wind seeped around the edges in a high-pitched whine. Tink sniffed at her legs, assuring himself she was okay, then barked at the door.

Hope pushed her hair out of her face and blew out a deep breath. That was a full-fledged blizzard, a complete white out, where the wind whipped the snow around and blotted out visibility. Her shoulder ached where the door had hit her, and snow melted on her polished floor. "I won't do that again," she muttered, going in search of a mop and towel to dry the floor.

As she was cleaning up the water, the lights dimmed, then flickered brightly again. Ten seconds later they went off.

Having expected it, she had a flashlight close to hand, and switched it on. For a moment the house was eerily silent, then the generator automatically switched on and in the kitchen the refrigerator hummed to life. Just that faint noise was enough to banish the alarming sense of being disabled.

Anticipating, Hope had put out the oil lamps. She lit the lamp on the mantel, then put the match to the dry kindling and rolled newspapers under the logs she had already laid. Small blue-and-yellow flames licked at the paper, then curled up the sticks of kindling. She watched the fire for a moment to make certain it had caught, then

259

moved around lighting the other lamps, turning the wicks low so they didn't smoke. Normally she wouldn't have lit so many lamps, but normally she wasn't alone, either. She had never thought herself timid and she wasn't afraid of the dark, but something about being alone in a blizzard was a little unnerving.

Tink settled down on his rug, his muzzle resting on his front paws. Perfectly content, he closed his eyes.

"You shouldn't get so worked up," Hope advised the dog, and he responded by rolling onto his side and stretching out.

Television reception had been nonexistent all afternoon, and the radio was picking up mostly static. She had turned it off earlier but now switched it over to battery operation and turned it on again, hoping the reception was better. It wasn't. Sighing, she switched it off. Why, at this rate, it might be a couple of days before she learned there was a blizzard.

It was too early to go to bed; she felt as if she should be doing something, but didn't know what. Restlessly she prowled around, the shrill whistle of the wind getting on her nerves. Maybe a bath would help. She climbed the stairs, peeling out of her clothes as she went. Already the heat was intensifying upstairs, and because her bedroom door was open, that room was toasty.

Instead of showering, she ran a tub of water and lolled in it, her blond hair pinned on top of her head and the mellow light of a lamp flickering over her. Her naked flesh gleamed in the water, oddly different in lamplight; the curves were highlighted and shadows deepened, so that her breasts looked more voluptuous, the hair between her legs darker and more mysterious.

It wasn't a bad body, for thirty-one, she thought as she inspected herself. In fact, it was a damn good body. Hard work kept her slim and toned. Her breasts weren't large, but they were high and well-shaped; her belly was flat, and she had a nice butt.

It was a body that hadn't had sex in five long years.

Immediately she winced away from the thought. As much as she had enjoyed making love with Dylan, on the whole she wasn't tormented by horniness. For a couple of years after his death she hadn't felt even the slightest flicker of sexual need. That had gradually changed, but not to the extent that she felt frustrated enough to do something about it. Now, however, her loins clenched with a sharp surge of need. Maybe the tub bath had been a mistake, the warm water lapping at her naked body, too much like a touch, a caress.

Tears stung her eyes and she closed them, leaning back and sinking even deeper into the water, letting it envelop her. She wanted sex. Hard-thrusting, sweaty, heart-pounding sex. And she wanted to love again, to *be* loved again. She wanted that closeness, that warmth, to be able to reach out in the night and know she wasn't alone. She wanted a baby. She wanted to waddle around with bloated breasts and an extended belly, her bladder under constant pressure, feeling their child squirming within her.

Oh, she wanted.

She allowed five minutes for a pity party, then sniffed and briskly sat up, using her toes to open the drain. Standing, she pulled the curtains closed and turned on the shower, rinsing away both soap and the blues.

Maybe she didn't have a man, but she did have nice, thick flannel pajamas, and she put them on, reveling in their warmth and comfort. Flannel pajamas possessed the same powers of reassurance as a hot bowl of soup on a cold day, a subliminal "there, there."

After brushing her teeth and hair, moisturizing her face, and pulling on an extra-thick pair of socks, she felt considerably better. Indulging in a hot bath, the sniffles, and a bout of self-pity was something she hadn't done in a long time, and it had been way overdue. Now that the ritual was behind her, she felt ready to deal with a blizzard.

Tink was lying at the foot of the stairs, waiting for her. He wagged a greeting, then stretched out in front of the bottom step so she had to step over him. "You could move," she informed him, as she did on a regular basis. He never took the hint, assuming it was his right to lie wherever he wanted.

After the warmth of the upstairs, the downstairs felt chilly. She poked up the fire, then microwaved herself a cup of hot chocolate. With the chocolate, a book, and a small battery-operated reading light, she installed herself on the couch. Cushions behind her back and a throw over her legs added the perfect touch. Soothed, pampered, comfortable, she lost herself in the book.

The night hours drifted by. She dozed, woke, eyed the clock on the mantel: ten-fifty. She should go to bed, she thought, but getting up so she could lie down again seemed ridiculous. On the other hand, she had to get up anyway to tend the fire, which was low.

Yawning, she added a couple of logs to the fire. Tink came over to watch, and Hope scratched behind his ears. Suddenly he stiffened, his ears lifting, and a growl rumbled in his throat. He tore over to the front door and stood in front of it, barking furiously.

Something was out there.

She didn't know how Tink could hear anything over the howl of the wind, but she trusted the acuity of his senses. She had a pistol in the drawer of her nightstand, but that was upstairs and her father's rifle was much closer. Running into the bedroom, her socks sliding on the polished floor, she grabbed the rifle from its rack and the box of bullets from the shelf below it. Carrying both out into the great room where she could see, she racheted five bullets into place.

Between the wind and Tink's barking, she couldn't hear anything else. "Tink, quiet!" she commanded. "C'mere, boy." She patted her thigh, and with a worried look at the door, Tink trotted over to stand beside her. She stroked his head, whispering praise. He growled again, every muscle in his body tense as he shoved in front of her and pushed against her legs.

Was that a thump on the porch? Straining her ears, patting Tink so he would be quiet, she tilted her head and listened. The wind screamed.

Her mind raced, running through the possibilities. A bear? Normally they would be in their dens by now, but the weather had been mild. Cougar, wolf . . . they would avoid humans and a house, if possible; could a blizzard make them desperate enough for shelter that the shy, wary animals would ignore their instincts?

Something thumped against the door, hard. Tink tore away from her, charging at the door, barking his head off again.

Hope's heart was pounding, her hands sweating. She wiped her palms on her pajamas and gripped the rifle more securely. "Tink, be quiet!"

He ignored her, barking even louder as another thump came, this one hard enough to rattle the door. Oh, God, was it a bear? The door would probably hold, but the windows wouldn't, not if the animal was determined to get in.

"Help."

She froze, not certain she had heard the muffled word. "Tink, shut up!" she yelled, and the tone of her voice briefly silenced the dog.

She hurried over to the door, the rifle ready in her hands. "Is anyone out there?" she called.

Another thump, much weaker, and what sounded like a groan.

"Dear God," she whispered, transferring the rifle to one hand and reaching to unbolt the door. There was a *person* out in this weather. She hadn't even considered that possibility, because she was so far from a main road. Anyone who left the protection of their vehicle shouldn't have been able to make it to her house, not in these conditions.

She opened the door and something white and heavy crashed into her legs. She screamed, staggering back. The door crashed against the wall, and the wind blew snow all over the floor, then sucked the warmth from the cabin with its icy breath.

The white thing on her floor was a man.

Hope set the rifle aside and grabbed him under

the arms. She braced her legs, trying to drag him across the threshold so she could shut the door, and grunted as she moved him only a few inches. Damn, he was heavy! Ice pellets stung her face like bees, and the wind was unbelievably cold. She closed her eyes against the onslaught and braced herself for another effort. Desperation gave her strength; she threw herself backward, hauling the man with her. She fell, his weight pinning her to the floor, but his legs were over the threshold.

Tink was beside himself with worry, barking and lunging, then whining. He thrust his muzzle at her face for a quick lick of reassurance, for her or himself she couldn't begin to guess; then he sniffed at the stranger and resumed barking. Hope gathered herself for one more effort, and pulled the man all the way inside.

Panting, she crawled over to the door and wrestled it shut. The wind hammered at it, as if enraged at being shut out. She could feel the heavy door shuddering under the onslaught. Hope secured the bolt, then turned her attention to the man.

He had to be in bad shape. Frantically she knelt beside him, brushing away snow and ice that crusted his clothes and the towel he had wrapped over his face.

"Can you hear me?" she asked insistently. "Are you awake?"

He was silent, limp, not even shivering, which wasn't a good sign. She pushed back the hood of his heavy coat and unwrapped the towel from his face, then used it to wipe the snow from his eyes. His skin was white with cold, his lips blue. From the waist down, his clothes were wet and coated with a sheet of ice.

As swiftly as possible, given his size and the difficulty of wrestling an unconscious man out of wet clothing that had been frozen stiff, she began undressing him. Thick gloves came off first, then the coat. She didn't take the time to inspect his fingers for frostbite, but moved down to his feet and began unlacing the insulated boots, then tugged them off. He wore two pairs of socks, and she peeled them away. His feet were icy. Moving back up, she began unbuttoning his shirt and only then noticed that he wore a deputy sheriff's uniform, the shirt stretched tight across his chest and shoulders.

Under the shirt he wore a thermal pullover,

and under that a T-shirt. He had been prepared for cold weather, but not for being caught out in it. Maybe his vehicle had slid off the road, though she didn't see how he could have made his way such a distance under these drastic conditions. It was nothing less than a miracle, or sheer chance, that he'd managed to stumble onto the house. By all logic, he should be dead out in the snow. And unless she could get him warm, he might yet die.

She tossed the three shirts into a heap, then attacked his belt buckle. It was coated with ice, the belt itself frozen stiff. Even the zipper of his fly was iced over. Unable to see in the storm, he must have stepped into the lake; the wonder was that he had managed to stay on his feet and not completely submerge himself. If he had gone under and gotten his head wet, he wouldn't have been able to make it to the house; most of the body's heat was lost through the scalp surface.

She fought the stiff fabric, using sheer force to get his pants off. The thermal underwear underneath was even more difficult, because it clung. Finally he lay on her floor in a puddle of melting snow and ice, clad only in his white shorts. She thought to leave them on, but they were wet too, and getting him warm was more important than preserving his modesty. She stripped them down his legs and tossed them onto the pile of wet clothes.

Now she had to get him dried off and wrapped up. She ran to the downstairs bathroom and gathered up some towels, and then stripped the blankets off her father's bed. She raced back. The man hadn't moved from his sprawled position on the floor. She dragged him out of the puddle, hastily dried him, then spread a blanket on the floor and rolled him onto it. Wrapping it around him, she then dragged him in front of the fire. Tink sniffed at him, whined, then lay down beside him.

"That's right, boy, snuggle close," Hope whispered. Her muscles were trembling with exertion, but she ran to the kitchen and stuffed one of the towels into the microwave. When she got it out, the cloth was so hot she could barely hold it.

She raced back to the great room and wrapped the hot towel around the man's head. Then, grimly, she stripped off her own clothes. She was naked beneath her pajamas, but when this man's life depended on how fast she could get him warm, she wasn't about to waste time running upstairs to put on underwear. Grabbing up the other blanket, she held it in front of the fire until it was toasty. Throwing open the blanket wrapped around the man, she placed the warm blanket over him, tucking it around his cold feet; then she slid under it with him.

Shared body heat was the best way to combat hypothermia. Hope pressed herself close to his cold body, forcing herself not to flinch as his icy skin touched hers. Oh, God, he was so cold. She got on top of him, put her arms around him, pressed her warm face to his. She massaged his arms and shoulders, tucked his hands under her belly, cupped her hands over his ears until they warmed. She slid her feet up and down his legs, stroking away the cold, massaging the blood through his veins.

He moaned, a faint sound whispering past his parted lips.

"That's right," she murmured. "Wake up, sweetie." She stroked his face, his beard stubble scraping across her palm. His lips weren't as blue, she thought.

The towel around his head had cooled. Hope unwrapped it and slipped out from under the blanket, then ran to the kitchen and reheated the towel in the microwave. Back to the great room, put the towel around his head, crawl under the blanket with him again. He was tall, and she wasn't; she couldn't reach all of him at once. She slid down and warmed his feet with hers, curling her toes over his until his flesh caught some of her body heat.

Slithering back up his body, she lay on top of him again. He was hard with muscle, and that was good, because muscles generated heat.

He began to shiver.

3

Hope held him, murmuring to him, trying to get him to talk to her. If she could get him awake enough to drink some coffee, the heat and caffeine would go a long way toward rousing him, but trying to pour hot coffee into an unconscious man was a good way to both choke him and burn him.

He moaned again, and sucked in a quick breath. He made a sharp movement with his head, dislodging the towel. The heat had dried his hair; it was dark, glistening with bronze lights in the glow of the fire. Hope tucked the towel back around his head to keep him from losing any of the precious body heat he had gained, and stroked his forehead, his cheeks. "Wake up, honey. Open your eyes and talk to me." She whispered to him, unconsciously using endearments to both reassure him and entice him to respond. Tink's ears perked up, because he was accustomed to that sweet tone being used when she spoke to him. He moved down to the man's feet, crowding against them when he lay down again. Maybe he could feel their chill through the blanket; with his thick fur, that would feel good to him. Or maybe it was instinct that led him to warm the man. Hope talked to Tink too, telling him what a good dog he was.

The faint, occasional shivers began to intensify. They wracked the man's body, roughening his skin, contorting his muscles. His teeth clenched and began chattering.

Hope held him through the convulsive shaking. He was in pain, barely conscious, groaning and breathing hard. He tried to curl into a ball, but she held him too tightly. "You're all right," she kept telling him. "Wake up, please. Open your eyes."

Unbelievably, he obeyed. His lids half lifted. His eyes were glazed, unfocused. Then they closed again, dark lashes resting on his cheeks. His arms

swept up and locked around her, desperately clinging to her warmth as he was wracked by another
bout of uncontrollable shaking. His entire body
was tense, shuddering.

He was as strong as an ox; his arms were like
steel bands around her. She murmured soothingly
to him, rubbing his shoulders, pressing as close to
him as she could. His skin definitely felt warmer
now. *She* was hot, sweating from exertion and
being swaddled in the heated blanket. She was
exhausted from the effort of dragging him inside
and wrestling him out of his clothes, as well as
from the stress of knowing he would die if she
didn't get him warm.

He relaxed beneath her, the bout of shivering
over. He was breathing hard. He moved restlessly,
shifting his legs, shrugging the towel away from
his head. The towel seemed to annoy him, so she
didn't replace it. Instead she folded it and lifted
his head to slide the towel underneath, giving him
more padding between his head and the hard
floor.

At first he had been too cold, and the situation
too urgent, for her to notice, but for some
moments now she had been growing more aware

of the sensations produced by his naked body against hers. He was a tall, well-built man, with a nice hairy chest and even nicer hard muscles. Good-looking too, now that his features weren't pinched and blue. Her nipples tingled from the rasping of his chest hair, and Hope knew it was time to get up. She pushed gently against him, trying to rise, but he groaned and tightened his arms, shivering again, so she let herself relax.

The shaking wasn't as violent this time. He swallowed and licked his lips, and his eyes flickered open again, just for a second. Then he seemed to doze, and because he was warm now, Hope wasn't alarmed. Her own muscles quivered from exhaustion. She closed her eyes too, resting for just a minute.

Time drifted. Half-asleep, warm, boneless from fatigue, she didn't know if a minute had passed, or an hour. His hand moved down to her bottom, curving over one rounded cheek. He shifted beneath her, muscled legs moving, sliding between her thighs. His engorged penis prodded at her exposed opening.

It happened so fast that he was inside her before she was fully awake. He rolled, pinning her beneath him on the blanket, mounting her, squeezing his penis into her and driving it deep with quick, hard shoves. After five years of chastity the penetration hurt, stretching her around his thick shaft, but it felt good too. Disoriented, unbelievably aroused, Hope arched her hips and felt him prod deeply, nudging her cervix. She cried out, gasping, her neck arching back as the sensation rocketed through her nerve endings.

There was no finesse, no lingering arousal. He simply began thrusting, his heavy weight holding her down, and she wound her arms and legs around him and met his thrusts with mindless ones of her own. In the mellow light of fire and lamp she saw his face, his eyes open now, very blue and still dazed, his expression set in the hardness of physical absorption. He was operating solely on animal instinct, his body aroused by the closeness of hers, by the naked intimacy that had been necessary to save his life. He was aware only of being warm and alive, and of her bare body in his arms.

On a purely physical level, the pleasure was more intense than any she had ever known. She had never felt more female, never been so acutely aware of her own body, or of the hard masculinity of a man's. She felt every inch of his smooth, hard shaft as he rocked back and forth inside her, felt the excited, welcoming cling of her inner flesh as each stroke took her closer and closer to climax. She was unbearably hot, her skin scorching, trembling pleasure lingering just out of reach. She grabbed his buttocks, holding him tight and grinding herself as deeply onto him as she could, crying out as the already intense pleasure became even more so. He gave a hoarse cry and convulsed, bucking, hips pumping, spurting hot semen, and Hope dissolved on an agonizing pulse of sensation.

He sank down on her, trembling in every muscle, his heart pounding violently, his breathing hard and fast. As shaken and dazed as he, she put her arms around him and held him close.

Unbelievably, they slept. Wrung out, emptied, hollowed, she felt the darkness descending on her and could do nothing to resist it. He was limp and heavy on top of her, already asleep. She managed to touch his cheek, stroke his dark hair back from his forehead, and then surrendered to the overwhelming need for rest.

THE COLLAPSE OF A LOG woke her. She stirred, wincing as her muscles protested the hard floor beneath her, the heavy body weighing her down. Confused, at first she thought she was dreaming. This couldn't be real, she couldn't be lying naked on the floor with a strange man, who was also completely naked.

But Tink was snoozing in his accustomed place, and the howling wind, the gently flickering lamplight, recalled the blizzard. Everything clicked into place.

And just as abruptly she realized he was also awake. He was lying very still, but every muscle was tense, and the penis still nestled inside her was growing thicker and longer by the second.

If she was confused, she could only imagine how disoriented he was. Gently she touched his back, smoothing her palm up the muscled expanse. "I'm awake," she murmured, her touch telling him she was there because she wanted to be, that everything was okay.

He lifted his head, and their eyes met. She felt an almost tangible shock as she stared into those blue eyes, eyes that were completely aware and revealed the sharpness of the personality behind them, as well as his comprehension of the situation.

Hope blushed. Her cheeks heated and she almost groaned aloud. What should she say to a man she was meeting for the first time, when she was lying naked beneath him and his erection was firmly lodged inside her?

He trailed one fingertip across her lips, then lightly stroked her hot cheek. "Do you want me to stop?" he whispered.

The first time had caught her unawares, but Hope was always brutally honest with herself, and she didn't allow herself to pretend she had been unwilling. This time, however, they were both fully cognizant of what they were doing. She didn't stop to analyze or question her response; she simply gave it. "No," she whispered in return. "Don't stop."

He kissed her then, a kiss as gentle and searching as if nothing had ever passed between them, as if he wasn't already inside her. He wooed her as if it were the first time, kissing her for a long time until her mouth slanted eagerly under his, until their tongues twined together. His hands were tender on her breasts, learning how she liked to be touched, teasing her nipples into tight peaks. He stroked her belly, her hips, between her legs. He licked his fingertips and stroked them over the ultrasensitive bud of her clitoris, drawing it out, make her gasp and arch her hips upward. He grunted at the resulting sensation as she took him even deeper.

She thought she would die from sensual torment before he finally began moving, but she enjoyed it so much she didn't urge him to hurry. She hadn't realized how hungry she was for this, for a man's attention, for his body, for the exquisite release of lovemaking. Even her frustration earlier, in the bath, hadn't prepared her for her total surrender to sensuality. She reveled in every kiss, every touch, every stroke. She clung to him and returned the caresses, trying to return some of the pleasure he was giving her, and judging from his groans she succeeded.

The time came when they no longer needed the gentle touches, when nothing mattered but the pounding drive to orgasm. Hope let herself get lost in the urgency of the moment, let her body drown in pure pleasure . . . and then he aroused her again, whispering, "Let me feel it again, let me feel you come."

His self-control held, barely. When the pulses of her third climax began, he made a deep, helpless sound in his throat and shuddered over her.

This time she didn't allow herself the luxury of sleep. This time he gently withdrew and collapsed on the blanket beside her. His hand sought hers, clasping her fingers against his callused palm.

"Tell me what happened," he finally said, his voice low and even. "Who are you?"

An introduction at this point seemed unbearably awkward. Hope blushed again, and cleared her throat. "Hope Bradshaw."

The blue eyes searched her face. "Tanner. Price Tanner."

The fire was getting too low. She needed to put another couple of logs on, but getting up and standing naked in front of him was somehow impossible. She looked around for her pajamas and, in an agony of embarrassment, realized she needed to bathe before putting them on.

He saw where she was looking, and he didn't suffer any such modesty. Unfolding his long length from the floor, he stepped over to the stack of wood and replenished the fire. Hope did exactly what she had been embarrassed to let him do to her, looked him over good, from head to foot. She liked what she saw, every inch of him. His muscles were delineated in the firelight, revealing the slope and curve of broad shoulders, wide chest, the long bulge of strong thigh muscles. His buttocks were round, firm. Even flaccid, his penis was intriguingly thick, and his testicles swung heavily below them. *Price Tanner.* She repeated his name in her mind, the syllables strong and brisk.

Tink looked a little grumpy at having had his sleep disturbed. He got up and sniffed at the stranger, and wagged his tail when the man leaned down and patted him. "I remember the dog barking," Price Tanner said.

"He heard you before I did. His name is Tinkerbell. Tink, for short."

"Tinkerbell?" He glanced at her, blue eyes incredulous. "He's gay?"

Hope sputtered with laughter. "No, he's just an eternally optimistic, goofy dog. He thinks the world is here to pet him."

"He may be right." He studied the sodden mass of his clothing, the water puddled on the floor. "How long have I been here?"

She looked at the clock. Two-thirty. "Three and

283

a half hours." Too much had happened in such a short length of time, and yet she felt as if only an hour or so had passed instead of almost twice that. "I dragged you in and got you out of your clothes. You must have stepped into the lake, because you were wet from the waist down. I dried you off and wrapped you in a blanket."

"Yeah, I remember going into the water. I knew this place was here, but I couldn't see a damn thing."

"I don't know how you made it this far. Why were you on foot? Did you have an accident? And why were you out in this weather anyway?"

"I was trying to make it down to Boise. The Blazer slid off the road and broke out the windshield, so I couldn't stay there. Like I said, I knew this place was here, and I had a compass. I didn't have much choice except try to get here."

"You're a walking miracle," she said frankly. "Logically, you should be dead out in the snow."

"But I'm not, thanks to you." He returned to the blanket and stretched out beside her, his gaze somber. He caught a tendril of blond hair, rubbing it between his fingers before smoothing it behind her ear. "I know when you got under the blanket to get me warm, you weren't expecting me to jump you as soon as I was half conscious. Tell me the truth, Hope: Were you willing?"

She cleared her throat. "I—I was *surprised*." She touched his hand. "I wasn't unwilling. Couldn't you tell?"

He briefly closed his eyes in relief. "I don't have a real clear memory of anything that happened until I woke up on top of you. Or rather, I remember what I did and what *I* felt, but I wasn't sure you felt the same." He spread his hand on her belly and lightly stroked upward to cover her breast. "I thought maybe I'd lost my head, waking up with such a pretty, brown-eyed little blonde naked next to me."

"Strictly speaking, I wasn't *next* to you. I was on top of you." Her face got hot again. Damn those blushes! "It seemed the best way to get you warm."

"It worked," he said, and for the first time a smile curved his mouth.

Hope almost lost her breath. He was ruggedly attractive rather than handsome, but when he smiled, her heart did a crazy loop. It must be chemistry, she thought dazedly. She had seen

285

many better-looking men; Dylan had been better looking, in a clean-cut, classical way. But what her eyes saw and her body felt were two different things, and she had never experienced such a strong sexual response to any other man. She wanted to make love again, and before she gave in to the need, she forced herself to remember he had been through a harrowing, physically exhausting ordeal.

"Do you want some coffee?" she asked hurriedly, getting to her feet. She carefully didn't look at him as she gathered up her pajamas. "Or something to eat? I made a big pot of stew yesterday. Or how about a hot bath? The water heater is wired to the generator, so there's plenty of hot water."

"That sounds good," he said, also standing. "All of it." He reached out and caught her arms, turning her so she faced him. Bending his head, he gave her another of those sweet, tender kisses. "I also want to make love to you again, if you'll let me."

Nothing like this had ever happened to her before. Hope looked up at him. Her heart did another crazy loop, and she knew she wasn't going to call a halt to this now. For as long as the blizzard lasted, she and Price Tanner were together, and she might never have another chance like this.

"I'd like that too," she managed to say.

"Maybe on a bed instead of the floor?" He circled her nipple with his thumb, making it harden and stand erect.

"Upstairs." She swallowed. "It's warm up there, because all the heat rises. I couldn't get you up the stairs, though, so I put you in front of the fireplace."

"I'm not complaining." He tugged the pajamas from her arms and let them drop to the floor. "On second thought, let's forget the coffee and the stew. The bath too, unless you planned to be in the tub with me."

She hadn't, but it was a darn good idea. She went into his arms, forgetting everything except the earthy magic their bodies made together.

4

Hope woke beside him in the morning and lay watching him sleep, her body more deeply contented than she could remember it ever being before. She didn't wonder how or why she responded so strongly to a man about whom she knew little more than his name; she simply accepted the joy this chance encounter had brought her. The warmth of his body made the bed a cozy nest she didn't want to leave, especially since the chill in the room told her the fire in the fireplace had burned out.

It had been so long since she had been able to enjoy such a simple pleasure as lying beside a sleeping man, listening to the slow, deep rhythm of his breathing. She wanted to cuddle close to him, but was reluctant to wake him. He was sleeping deeply, evidence of his exhaustion. After nearly freezing to death, he hadn't exactly spent a restful night.

One muscled arm lay draped over the pillow, and she could see the dark bruises on his wrist. On top of everything else, he had been in a car accident. The wonder wasn't that he slept now, but that he had been so energetic during the night.

She surveyed the other details available to her. He had beautiful hair, dark and thick, with streaks of bronze glinting through it as if he spent a lot of time in the sun. His face was turned toward her in his sleep, and she smiled, wanting to trace her finger along the bridge of his nose, which was high and a little crooked, maybe as the result of a fight. His mouth was wide and well-shaped, his lips soft. His jaw was angular, his chin nothing less than stubborn. Good-looking, rugged, attractive; definitely not handsome, as she had noticed before. Just looking at him made her breasts tighten.

She felt almost dizzy from the force of her attraction to him. She had forgotten how heady infatuation could be, and how powerful. If she had met him under normal circumstances, no doubt she would still have been attracted to him; but without the overwhelming physical intimacy that had been forced between them, she might not even have encouraged him. The necessary contact of their nude bodies, however, had established a link even before he had regained consciousness. She had stroked him, knew the textures of his skin, from the roughness of his beard-stubbled cheeks to the sleekness of his muscular shoulders. Her nipples had been tight from rubbing against his chest, her legs had tangled with his, and though she hadn't touched him sexually, she had inescapably felt his genitals against her own. She hadn't let herself think about it, but nevertheless she had been almost unbearably aroused.

Her sexual attraction wasn't due to simple deprivation. If she had thought it was, before, now she knew differently, because she was certainly no longer deprived and she still felt the same. Their sexual fit was devastating in its perfection. It was as if he had been born knowing exactly how to touch her, as if his body had been crafted specifically to bring her maximum pleasure.

She thought it must be the same, at least sexually, for him. As exhausted and drained as he had to have been, still he had turned to her time and again, his hands literally shaking with need as he drew her under him.

Her breath sighed gently, rapidly, between her lips.

The wind still blew, rattling the windows. She couldn't see anything beyond the glass but an impenetrable white curtain. While the blizzard raged, the world couldn't intrude, and he was hers.

What a difference one day made. Yesterday she had been panicked by the sense of time passing her by, thinking she had lost all opportunity to get out of life what she had always wanted most—a family. Then Price Tanner had blown in on a snowstorm, and abruptly the future was bright with promise.

He was a deputy. He had said he was heading to Boise, so he could be from there, but he had known the resort was here, which meant he was familiar with the area, so he might be local. She would ask him when he woke.

Despite the heady lovemaking of the night, and more she hoped to enjoy while he was here, she was afraid to automatically assume they were a couple. The circumstances that had brought them together were extreme, and once the weather cleared he might be on his way without a backward look. She had known that from the beginning, and accepted that risk. She, who had never had any lover other than her husband, had gone into this with her eyes open.

If this situation between them grew into something permanent, she would be happy beyond belief. She didn't let herself think the word "love," for how could she love someone she didn't really know? He was a tender, generous lover, and during the night she had seen signs of a sharp sense of humor, both qualities she liked, but she was too cautious to imagine either of them were in love.

The truth was, she had seized the opportunity to have a child.

Even beyond her own powerful attraction to him, the physical pleasure he had given her, she had been acutely aware of the lack of birth control. She hadn't taken birth control pills in five years, and there wasn't a condom in the house. She was a healthy, fertile woman, the odds were he was equally fertile, and the time was roughly right. He had climaxed inside her five times during the night, with no barrier—chemical, hormonal, or otherwise—between her and his sperm, and the knowledge was so erotic she trembled with need.

This morning, her head clear and the stresses of the emergency behind her, she felt guilty about what she had done. She didn't even know if he was married! He didn't wear a ring, and the thought hadn't occurred to her the night before. She cringed inside at the thought of sleeping with a married man and didn't want to think how much it would hurt if he did turn out to be an unfaithful jerk. But even assuming he was unmarried, the hard truth was she hadn't had any right to take such an enormous step without his consent. He hadn't asked about birth control, but he had been through quite an ordeal and could be excused for having other things on his mind, such as being alive.

She felt as if she had stolen his free will from

him. If she did get pregnant, he might be, justifiably, very angry. If there was such a thing as unauthorized use of sperm, then she had committed the offense.

Being a single mother wouldn't be easy, assuming she had gotten pregnant. If she had given herself time to think about it, caution would have prevented her from taking the chance. But she *hadn't* taken the time, Price hadn't given her the time, and all she could feel now was a guilty joy that a child might be the result of their lovemaking. Her father wouldn't like it, but he loved her, and it wasn't as if she was a teenager unable to support herself or her baby. She would prefer being married, but as she had so sharply realized the day before, time was running out. She had taken the chance.

Hope slid out of bed, careful not to waken him. Her thighs trembled, and she ached deep inside her body. Her first few steps were little more than a hobble, as long unused muscles and flesh protested their treatment during the night. Silently she gathered her clothes and tiptoed out of the room.

Tink trotted from the kitchen as she came

downstairs, his eagerness telling her she was late, he was hungry, but he forgave everything for the joy of her company. She poured some food into his bowl, then immediately went to rebuild the fire. It had burned down to embers, and the house was cold. She relaid the fire, the kindling catching immediately from the glowing embers, and carefully stacked three logs on the grate. Then she put on a pot of coffee and, while it was brewing, went into her father's bathroom and stepped into the shower. Thank God for hot water, because otherwise she couldn't have tolerated the cold!

The shower went a long way toward relieving her aches and pains. Feeling much better, she pulled on a pair of sweatpants and an oversize flannel shirt, put on two pairs of thick socks, and padded out to have her first cup of coffee.

Cup in hand, she went into the great room to mop up the water she had left puddled on the floor the night before and straighten Price's clothing.

The best way to dry them would be to hang them over the balcony railing, where the heat was. She hung his coat over a chair and set his boots beside the fireplace, because they needed to dry more slowly, but carried the rest of his clothes upstairs. Until Price's clothes dried, she supposed he would have to sit around naked. He was too tall for her father's clothes, and all she had left of Dylan's clothing was a couple of shirts she wore herself.

No—come to think of it, her dad had bought a pair of black sweatpants that had evidently had the wrong tag attached to them, because they were several inches too long for him. Returning them would have cost more in gasoline than the pants were worth, so he had just folded them away in the top of his closet. Buying by size being as iffy as it was, she was fairly certain she could lay her hands on an extra-large sweatshirt too.

She straightened out the uniform to minimize wrinkles and, as she was doing so, noticed a tear in the left pants leg. Lifting the garment for a closer inspection, she saw the faded red stain below the tear, as if whatever had made the tear had also brought blood. But she had undressed Price, and she knew he wasn't hurt anywhere. She frowned at the stain, then mentally shrugged and draped the pants over the railing.

Something was missing. She stared at the uniform for a moment before it hit her: where was his pistol? Had he lost it somewhere? But he didn't have a holster, either, so he must have taken the gun off and . . . left it in the Blazer? That didn't make sense. He didn't have a wallet with him, either, but that was easier to understand. It could have fallen out of his pocket at any time during his hazardous trek through the blinding snow; it might even be in the lake.

Even if he had lost the pistol, would he then have removed the gun belt and holster and left them behind? They were part of his uniform. Of course, who knew what shape he had been in when he left the Blazer? He could have hit his head and not realized it, though if he *had* been addled, it had taken an even bigger miracle than she had thought for him to find his way here.

Well, the missing pistol was only a small mystery, and one that would wait until he woke. The house was warming, the coffee was ready, and she was hungry.

Downstairs again, she picked up the phone just to check it, but the line was dead, not even static coming through. She turned on the radio and picked up the same thing—static. Given the conditions outside, she hadn't expected anything else, but she always checked periodically during power failures, just in case.

The rifle was where she had left it, propped beside the door. She retrieved it and returned it to the rack in her father's bedroom, before Tink knocked it down with an exuberant swish of his tail.

Carrying a cup of hot coffee with her, she then tidied the great room, putting the blankets and towels she had used in the laundry room to be washed whenever power returned. She cleaned up the puddles of melted snow and ice. Tink had been back and forth through the water several times, of course, leaving wet doggy tracks all over the house. She followed his trail, crawling on the floor and blotting up pawprints.

"I thought I smelled coffee."

Her head jerked up. He was standing at the balcony railing, his hair tousled, his jaw dark with beard stubble, his eyes still heavy-lidded from sleep. His voice was hoarse, and she wondered if he was getting sick.

"I'll bring a cup up to you," she said. "It's too

cold down here for you to be walking around without clothes."

"Then I think I'll stay right here. I'm not ready to be cold again, just yet." He gave her a crooked smile, and turned to pet Tink, who had bounded up the stairs as soon as he heard a new voice.

Hope went into her dad's room and searched until she found the long sweatpants. Then she collected a pair of shorts and some thick hunting socks, but try as she might she couldn't locate the extra-large sweatshirt she knew was here, somewhere. It was a gray University of Idaho shirt, and she had worn it once with leggings, but the thing had been so big she looked as if she were lost inside it. What had she done with it?

Maybe it was in the closet of the extra bedroom upstairs. She rotated her winter and summer clothing between that closet and the one in her room, but she didn't necessarily move everything.

With the small stack of clothes in her arms, she detoured to the kitchen and poured a cup of coffee, then carried everything up the stairs.

The roaring fire had rapidly warmed the upstairs. The bathroom door was open, and Price was in the shower. Hope set the cup on the vanity. "Here's your coffee."

He pulled the curtain aside and stuck his head out. Water streamed down his face. "Would you hand it to me, please. Thanks." He drank deeply, sighing as the caffeine jolted through him.

"I brought you some clothes. I hope you don't mind wearing my father's shorts."

"I don't if he doesn't." Blue eyes regarded her over the rim of the cup. "I'm glad you said they belonged to your father and not your husband. I didn't ask, last night, but I don't fool around with married women, and I sure do want to fool around some more with you."

"I'm a widow." She paused. "I had the same thoughts about you this morning. That I hadn't thought to ask if you were married, I mean."

"I'm not. Divorced, no kids." He took another sip of coffee. "So where is your father?" he asked, his tone casual.

"Visiting his brother in Indianapolis. Uncle Pete had a heart attack, and Dad flew out. He's supposed to be gone another week."

Price handed the cup back to her, smiling. "Think the blizzard will last another week?"

She laughed. "I doubt it." Both his wrists were bruised, she noticed.

"Damn. At least there's no question of leaving today, though I guess I should let some people know where I am."

"You can't. The phone lines are down too. I just checked."

"What rotten luck." The blue eyes twinkled as he pulled the shower curtain closed. "Marooned with a sexy blond." From behind the curtain came the sound of cheerful whistling.

Hope felt like whistling a tune herself. She listened to the wind blow and hoped it would be days before he would be able to leave.

She remembered something. "Oh, I meant to ask, are you hurt anywhere? I didn't see any blood last night, but your uniform is torn and has blood on it, or at least I think it's blood."

A few seconds lapsed before he answered. "No, I'm not hurt. I don't know what the stain is."

"Your pistol and holster are missing too. Do you remember what happened to them?"

Again there was a pause, and when he spoke, he sounded as if he had his face turned up to the spray. "I must have left them in the Blazer."

"Why would you have taken off your gun belt?"

"Damn if I know. Ah . . . do you have any weapons here? Other than the rifle I saw last night, that is."

"A pistol."

"Where do you keep it?"

"In my nightstand drawer. Why?"

"I might not be the only person to get stranded in the storm and come looking for shelter. It pays to be careful."

5

When he came downstairs, he was freshly shaved, with her father's borrowed razor, and he looked alert and vital in the sweat clothes she had provided. The big sweatshirt had been in the other closet after all, and it fit him perfectly, just loose enough to be comfortable.

She would normally have just eaten cereal, but with him there she was cooking a breakfast of bacon and eggs. He came up behind her as she stood at the island, turning bacon with a fork, and wrapped his arms around her waist. He kissed the top of her head, then rested his chin there. "I don't know which smells best, the coffee, the bacon, or you."

"Wow, I'm impressed. I must really smell good, if I rank up there with coffee and bacon."

She felt him grin, his chin moving on top of her head. "I could eat you right up." His tone was both teasing and serious, sensual, and a wave of heat that had nothing to do with embarrassment swept over her. She leaned back against him, her knees weak. He had a serious swelling in the groin area, and she rubbed her bottom against it.

"I think we need to go back to bed." There was no teasing at all in his voice this time.

"Now?"

"Now." He reached around her and turned off the cooktop.

Ten minutes later she was naked, breathless, trembling on the verge of climax. Her thighs were draped over his shoulders, and he was driving her, with his tongue, to absolute madness. She tried to pull him up and over her, but he pinned her wrists to the bed and continued what he was doing. She surrendered, her hips lifting, her body shuddering with completion. Only when she was limp did he move upward, covering her, sliding his erection into her with a smooth thrust that took him all the way in.

She inhaled deeply, having already forgotten how completely he filled her.

He began a gentle back-and-forth movement, gripping her shoulders, watching her face.

Guilt and her innate honesty nagged at her. "I'm not taking birth control pills," she blurted, knowing this wasn't exactly the best time to bring up her lack of protection.

He didn't stop. "I'm not wearing a rubber," he said equably. "I would stop, but that would be like closing the barn door after the horse is out, wouldn't it?"

Afterward, while she was in the bathroom, he finished dressing—again—and called out, "I'll go down and start breakfast again."

"I'll be there in a minute." She still felt incredibly weak-kneed, and relieved. She stared at her face in the mirror, her brown eyes huge. She was going to get pregnant. She knew it, sensed it. The prospect both terrified and exhilarated her. From now on, her life would be changed.

She went out into the bedroom and collected

her scattered garments, pulling them on again. After a lifetime of caution and careful behavior, taking such a deliberate risk was nerve-racking, like climbing on board a space shuttle without any previous training.

It pays to be careful, Price had said, but sometimes it paid to be careless too. And, anyway, she was doing this deliberately, not carelessly.

One of her socks had ended up between the bed and the nightstand. She got down on her knees to retrieve it, and because she was there, because she had just been remembering what Price had said, she opened the nightstand drawer to make certain the pistol was there.

It wasn't.

Slowly she stood, staring down at the empty drawer. She knew the pistol had been there. When her dad had left, she had checked to make certain it was loaded and returned it to the same place. Living in such an isolated place, where self-defense was sometimes necessary, she had learned how to use the weapon. Idaho had more than its share of dangerous wildlife, both animal and human. The ruggedness of the mountains, the isolation, seemed to be a magnet for nut groups, from neo-Nazis to drug runners. She might happen upon a bear or a cougar, but she was more worried about happening upon a human predator.

The pistol had been there, and now it wasn't. Price had asked where she kept it, not that finding it would have been that difficult. But why hadn't he simply said he wanted it close to hand? He was a cop; she understood that he was more comfortable armed than unarmed, especially when he wasn't on his own turf.

She went downstairs, her expression thoughtful. He was standing at the island, taking up the bacon. "Price, do you have my pistol?"

He slanted a quick, assessing look at her, then turned back to the bacon. "Yes."

"Why didn't you tell me you were getting it?"

"I didn't want to worry you."

"Why would I be worried?"

"What I said about other people coming here."

"*I* wasn't worried, but you seem to be," she said pointedly.

"It's my job to worry. I feel more comfortable armed. I'll put the pistol back if it bothers you."

She looked around. She didn't see the weapon lying on the cabinet. "Where is it?"

"In my waistband."

She felt uneasy, but she didn't know why. She herself had thought that he would feel more comfortable armed, and he had said so himself. It was just—for a moment, his expression had been . . . hard. Distant. Maybe it was because he worked in law enforcement and saw a lot of things the average person never even dreamed of seeing that he expected the worst. But for a moment, just for a moment, he had looked as dangerous as any of the scum with whom he dealt. He had been so easy and approachable until then that the contrast rattled her.

She shoved the uneasiness away and didn't say anything more about the pistol.

Over breakfast she asked, "In what county do you work?"

"This one," he said. "But I haven't been here long. Like I said, I knew this place was here, but I hadn't had time to get up here and meet you and your dad—and Tinkerbell, of course."

The dog, lying on the floor between their chairs in obvious hopes of doubling his chances of catching a stray tidbit, perked up when he heard his name.

"Table scraps aren't good for you," Hope said sternly. "Besides, you've already eaten."

Tink didn't look discouraged, and Price laughed.

"How long have you worked in law enforcement?"

"Eleven years. I worked in Boise before." His mouth quirked with amusement. "For the record, I'm thirty-four, I've been divorced eight years, I've been known to have a few drinks, and I enjoy an occasional cigar, but I'm not a regular smoker. I don't attend any church, but I believe in God."

Hope put down her fork. She could feel her face turning red in mortification. "I wasn't—"

"Yes you were, and I don't blame you. When a woman lets a man make love to her, she has a right to reassure herself about him, find out every detail right down to the size of his Fruit of the Looms."

"Jockeys," she corrected, and turned even redder.

He shrugged. "I just look at sizes, not brand names." The amusement turned into a grin. "Stop blushing. So you looked at my briefs; I looked at your panties this morning, didn't I? I bet you just hung mine over the railing to dry, instead of sniffing them the way I did yours."

He had sniffed, drawing an exaggeratedly deep breath and rolling his eyes in pretended ecstasy, making her laugh, before he had tossed the garment over his shoulder with a flourish.

"You were goofing around," she mumbled.

"Was I? Maybe I was turned on. What do you think? Was my dick hard?"

"It was hard before we went upstairs, so you can't use that argument."

"It got hard when I thought about sniffing your underwear."

She began to laugh, enjoying his teasing. She was beginning to suspect arguing with him would be like swatting at smoke.

"I do have a really bad habit," he confessed.

"Oh?"

"I'm addicted to remote controls."

"You and about a hundred million other men in America. We can pick up one station here— *one*—and when my dad watches television, he sits with the remote control in his hand."

"I don't think I'm that bad." He grinned and reached for her hand. "So, Hope Bradshaw, when

310

conditions are back to normal, will you go out to dinner with me?"

"Gee, I don't know," she said. "A date, huh? I don't know if I'm ready for that."

He chuckled and started to answer, but a sunbeam fell across their hands. Startled, they both looked at the light, then out the window. The wind had stopped blowing, and patches of blue sky were visible.

"I'll be damned," he said, getting up to walk to the window and look out. "I thought the storm would last longer than this."

"So did I," Hope said, her disappointment more intense than she wanted to show. He had asked her out, after all. The clearing weather meant he would be leaving sooner than she had anticipated, but it wasn't as if she wouldn't see him again.

She went over to the window too, and gasped when she saw the amount of snow. "Good heavens!" The familiar terrain was completely transformed, disguised by drifts of snow that appeared to level out the landscape. The wind had piled snow to window level on the porch.

"It looks like at least three feet. The ski resort

operators will love this, but it'll take the snow-plows a while to clear the roads." He walked to the door and opened it, and the frigidity of the air seemed to suck the warmth from the room. "Jesus!" He slammed the door. "The temperature has to be below zero. No chance of any of this melting."

Oddly, the improved weather seemed to make Price uneasy. As the day progressed, Hope noticed several times that he went from window to window, looking out, though he would stand to one side as he did so. She was busy, as being confined to the house didn't mean there weren't any chores to do, such as laundry, but doing it without electricity was twice as hard and took twice as long.

Price helped her wring out the clothes she had washed by hand, then braved the cold long enough to carry in more firewood while she hung the clothes over the stair railings to dry. She checked his uniform, picking up the shirt and feeling the seams, which would be the last to dry. Another hour would do it, she thought, as hot as Price was keeping the fire. The temperature on the second level had to be close to ninety.

She started to drape the shirt over the railing again when her attention was caught by the tag. The shirt was a size fifteen and a half. That was odd. She *knew* Price was bigger than that. The shirt had in fact been tight on him; she remembered how strained the buttons had been last night. Of course, he had been wearing a thermal shirt underneath, which would make the uniform seem tighter than it was. But if she had been buying a shirt for Price, she wouldn't have looked at anything smaller than a sixteen and a half.

He came in with a load of wood and stacked it on the fireplace. "I'm going to clear off the steps," he called up to her.

"That can wait until the weather's warmer."

"Now that the wind isn't blowing, it's bearable for a few minutes, and that's all it'll take to clear the steps." He buttoned his heavy coat and went back outside. At least he was wearing a pair of her dad's sturdy work gloves, and if his boots weren't completely dry, at least he had on three pairs of socks. Tink went with him, glad for the chance to do his business outside instead of on a pad.

With the weather clearing, perhaps she could pick up something on the radio now. Going downstairs, she switched it on; music filled the air, a welcome relief from static, and she listened to the song as she got the beef stew out of the refrigerator to warm it up for lunch.

The weather was the big news, of course, and as soon as the song ended the announcer began running down a list of closings. Her road was impassable, she heard, and the highway department estimated at least three days before all the roads in the county were cleared. Mail service was spotty, but utility crews were hard at work restoring service.

"Also in the news," the announcer continued, "a bus carrying six prisoners ran off County Road Twelve during the storm. Three people were killed, including two sheriff's deputies. Five prisoners escaped; two have been recaptured, but three are still at large. It is unknown if they survived the blizzard. Be alert for strangers in your area, as one of the prisoners is described as extremely dangerous."

Hope went still. The bottom dropped out of her stomach. County Road 12 was just a few miles away. She reached over and turned off the radio, the announcer's voice suddenly grating on her nerves.

She had to think. Unfortunately, what she was thinking was almost too frightening to contemplate.

Price's uniform shirt was too small for him. He didn't have a wallet. He had blown it off, but she was certain now that the stain on his pants leg was blood—and he had no corresponding wound. There were bruises on his wrists—from handcuffs? And he hadn't had a weapon.

He did now, though. Hers.

6

There was still the rifle. Hope left the stew sitting on the cabinet and went into her father's bedroom. She lifted the rifle from the rack, breathing a sigh of relief as the reassuring weight of it settled in her hands. Though she had loaded it just the night before, the lesson "always check your weapon" had been drilled into her so many times she automatically slid the bolt—and stared down into the empty chamber.

He had unloaded it.

Swiftly, she searched for the bullets; he had to have hidden them somewhere. They were too heavy to carry around, and he didn't have pockets in his sweat clothes anyway. But before she had time to look in more than a couple of places, she heard the door open, and she straightened in alarm. Dear God, what should she do?

Three prisoners were still at large, the announcer had said, but only one was considered extremely dangerous. She had a two-to-one chance that he wasn't the dangerous one.

But he had taken her pistol and unloaded the rifle—both without telling her. He had obviously taken the uniform off one of the dead deputies. Damn it, why hadn't the announcer warned people that one of the escaped prisoners could be wearing a deputy's uniform?

Price was too intelligent to get thrown in jail over some penny-ante crime, and if by some chance he had, he wouldn't compound the offense by escaping. The common criminal was, by and large, uncommonly stupid. Price was neither common nor stupid.

Given her own observations, she now thought her estimated chance of being snowbound with an extremely dangerous escaped criminal had just flip-flopped. What could "extremely dangerous" mean other than he was a murderer? A criminal didn't get that description hung on him by taking someone's television.

"Hope?" he called.

Hastily she returned the rifle to the rack, trying to be as quiet as she could. "I'm in Dad's room," she called, "putting up his underwear." She opened and closed a dresser drawer for the sound effect, then plastered a smile on her face and stepped to the door. "Are you about frozen?"

"Cold enough," he said, shrugging out of his coat and hanging it up. Tink shook about ten pounds of snow off his fur onto the floor, then came bounding over to Hope to say hello after his extended absence of ten minutes.

Automatically she scolded him for getting the floor wet again, though bending over to pet him probably ruined the effect. She went to get the broom and mop, hoping her expression didn't give her away. Her face felt stiff from strain; any smile she attempted must look like a grimace.

What could she do? What options did she have?

At the moment, she wasn't in any danger, she didn't think. Price didn't know she had been listening to the radio, so he didn't feel threatened.

He had no reason to kill her; she was providing him with food, shelter, and sex.

Her face went white. She couldn't bear having him touch her again. She simply couldn't.

She heard him in the kitchen, getting a cup of coffee to warm himself. Her hands began shaking. Oh, God. She hurt so much she thought she would fly apart. She had never been more attracted to a man in her life, not even Dylan. She had warmed him with her body, saved his life; in some primitive, basic way he was hers now. In just twelve short hours he had become the central focus of her mind and emotions, and that she didn't yet dare call it love was an effort at self-protection—too late. Part of her was being ripped away, and she didn't know if she could survive the agony. She might—dear God—she might even be pregnant with his child.

He had laughed with her, teased her, made love to her. He had been so tender and considerate that, even now, she couldn't describe it as anything except making love. Of course, Ted Bundy had been an immensely charming man too, except to the women he raped and murdered. Hope had always thought herself a fairly good judge of character, and everything Price had shown her so far said he was a decent and likable person, the type of man who coached Little League teams and danced a mean two-step. He had even, good-humoredly, given her his "stats" and asked her out on a date, just as if he would be around for a long time, be part of her life.

Either it was just a big game to him, or he was totally delusional. She remembered the moment when his expression had suddenly altered to something hard and frightening, and she knew he wasn't delusional.

He was dangerous.

She had to turn him in. She knew it, accepted the necessity, and the pain was so sharp she almost moaned aloud. She had always wondered why women would aid their husbands or boyfriends in eluding the law, and now she knew why; the thought of Price in jail for most of his life, perhaps even facing a death penalty, was devastating. And yet she wouldn't be able to live with herself if she did nothing and someone else died because she let him go.

Maybe she was wrong. Maybe she was jumping to the most ludicrous conclusion of her lifetime. The radio announcer hadn't said *all* the deputies on the bus had been killed, but that two of them had. On the other hand, neither had he said that one of the deputies was missing, which surely would have been in the news if that was the case.

And now she was grasping at straws, and she knew it. The deputy's uniform drying on the railing was too small for Price, and there was no logical reason for him to have exchanged his own uniform for one that didn't fit. Price was one of the escaped prisoners, not a deputy.

She had to keep him from knowing she knew about the bus wreck. She didn't have to worry about anything being on the television until the electric power was restored, and the next time he went to the bathroom, she would take the batteries out of the radio and hide them. All she had to do was periodically check the phone and, when service to it was restored, wait for the opportunity to call the sheriff's department.

If she kept her wits about her, everything would be all right.

"Hope?"

She jumped, her heart thundering with panic.

Price was standing in the door, watching her, his gaze sharp. She fumbled with the broom and mop and almost dropped them. "You startled me!"

"So I see." Calmly he stepped forward and took the broom and mop from her hands. Hope took an involuntary step back, fighting a sense of suffocation. He seemed even bigger in the small laundry room, his shoulders totally blocking the door. She had reveled in his size and strength when they were making love, but now she was overwhelmed by the thought of her utter helplessness in a physical match against him. Not that she had entertained any idea of wrestling him into submission, but she had to be prepared to fight him in any way possible, if necessary. Running would be the smartest thing to do, if she had the chance.

"What's wrong?" he asked. His expression was still, unreadable, and his gaze never left her face. He stood squarely in front of her, and there was no way past him, not in the narrow confines of the laundry room. "You look scared to death."

Considering how she must have looked, Hope knew she couldn't try to deny it; he would know she was lying. "I am," she confessed, her voice shaking. She didn't know what she was going to

say until the words began tumbling out. "I don't
. . . I mean, I've been widowed five years and I
haven't . . . I've just *met* you, and we—I—oh,
damn," she said helplessly, dwindling to an end.

His face relaxed, and a faint smile teased his
mouth. "So you just had one of those moments
when reality bites you on the ass, when you look
around and everything hits all at once and you
think, holy shit, what am I *doing?*"

She managed a nod. "Something like that," she
said, and swallowed.

"Well, let's see. You're caught alone in a blizzard, an almost dead stranger falls in your front
door, you save his life, and though you haven't
had a lover in five years, somehow he ends up on
top of you for most of the night. I can see how all
that would be a little disconcerting, especially
when you didn't use any birth control and might
have gotten pregnant."

Hope felt as if there were no blood left in her
face.

"Ah, honey." Gently he set the things aside and
caught her arms, his big hands rubbing up and
down as he eased her into his arms. "What happened, did you check the calendar and find out

323

getting pregnant is a lot more likely than you'd thought?"

Oh, God, she thought she might faint at his touch, the combined terror and longing so intense she couldn't bear it. How could he be so tender and comforting when he was a criminal, an escaped prisoner? And how could the feel of his strong body against hers be so right? She wanted to be able to rest her head on his shoulder and forget about the rest of the world, just stay with him here in these remote mountains where nothing could ever touch them.

"Hope?" He tilted his head so he could better see her face.

She gasped for breath, because she didn't seem to be getting enough oxygen. "The wrong time—is now," she blurted.

He took a deep breath too, as if reality had just taken a nip out of his ass too. "That close, huh?"

"On the money." She sounded a little steadier now, and she was grateful. The sharp edge of panic was fading. She had already decided she wasn't in any immediate danger, so she should just stay cool instead of jumping every time he came near. That would definitely make him suspicious, given how

willingly she had made love with him. She had
been lucky that his insightfulness had given her a
plausible reason for her upset, but at the same
time she had to remember exactly how sharp he
was. If he knew she had been listening to the
radio, it wouldn't take him five seconds to put it
all together and realize she was on to him.

"Okay." He blew out a breath. "Before, when
you told me you weren't on the pill, I didn't realize the odds. So what do you want to do? Stop
taking chances, or take our chances?" Suddenly,
impossibly, she felt him tremble. "Jesus," he said,
his voice shaking. "I've always been so fucking
careful, and vice versa."

"Do you feel reality nibbling?" Hope mumbled
against his chest.

"Nibbling, hell. I've got fang marks on my ass."
He trembled again. "The hell of it is . . . Hope—I
like the idea."

Oh, God. In despair, Hope pressed her face tight
against him. He couldn't be a killer, he simply
couldn't, not and treat her so sweetly, and tremble
at the thought of being a father. He would have to
have a split personality, to be both the man she
knew and the man she feared he could be.

"Your call," he said.

He was aroused. She could feel the hard bulge of his erection. Talking about the possibility of pregnancy hadn't scared him, it had turned him on, just the way she had felt earlier, knowing they were making love without protection. And her body was already so attuned to him, so responsive to his sexuality, that she felt the inner tightening of her own desire. She was shocked at herself, but helpless to kill her reaction. All she could do was refuse to satisfy her need.

Her mouth was dry from tension, and she tried to work up some saliva. "We—we should be careful," she managed to say, thankful he had given her this out. Even if he was one of the other escaped prisoners and not the one considered so dangerous, it would be criminally irresponsible of her to continue sleeping with him. She had already been irresponsible enough. She could live with what she had already done, but it couldn't continue.

"All right." Reluctantly he released her. His face was tense. "Call me when lunch is ready. I'm going to go shovel some more snow."

Hope stood where she was until she heard the

door slam behind him; then she covered her face with her hands and weakly sagged against the washing machine. Please, please, she prayed, let the telephone service be restored soon. She didn't know if she could stand another hour of this, much less *days*. She wanted to weep. She wanted to scream. She wanted to grab him and slam him against the wall and yell at him for being stupid and getting himself in trouble to begin with. Most of all, she wanted none of this to be true. She wanted to be completely mistaken in every conclusion she had reached.

She wanted Price.

7

While the stew was warming in the microwave, Hope took the batteries out of the radio and hid them in one of her lidded saucepans. She checked the phone, but wasn't surprised when she didn't hear a dial tone. The wind had died only a couple of hours ago, so the utility crews wouldn't have had a chance yet to begin work in her area; they would have to work behind the road crews.

The bus wreck, she thought, must have happened before the weather got so bad, otherwise no one would yet know about it. The authorities had had time to reach the scene and ascertain the two deputies were dead, as well as recapture two of the escaped prisoners. Price might not have eluded them if the blizzard hadn't interfered. The radio report had said the bus ran off the road during the storm, but what was reported wasn't always accurate, and the timing of events didn't really matter.

The microwave *ping*ed. Hope checked the stew, then set the timer for another two minutes. She could hear the thud of the shovel against the wooden porch, but Price was working on a section that wasn't in view of the windows.

If she could hear the shovel, could he have heard the radio earlier?

Sweat broke out on her forehead, and she sank weakly into a chair. Was he that good an actor?

This was making her crazy. The only way she could make it through was to stop second-guessing herself. It didn't matter whether Price was a murderer or a more ordinary criminal, she had to turn him in. She couldn't torment herself wondering what he knew or guessed, she had to proceed as best she could.

She thought of the rifle again and hastily left the chair to return to her father's bedroom, to search more thoroughly for the bullets. She couldn't afford to waste any of these precious minutes of privacy.

The box of cartridges wasn't in any of the bureau drawers. Hope looked around the room, hoping instinct would tell her the most likely hiding place—or the most unlikely. But the room was just an ordinary room, without secret panels or hidden drawers, or anything like that. She went to the bed and ran her hands under the pillows and mattress, but came up empty again.

She was pushing her luck by remaining any longer, so she hurried back to the kitchen and began setting the table. She had just finished when she heard Price stomping the snow off his boots, and the door opened.

"Damn, it's cold!" he said, shuddering as he shed his coat and sat down to pull off his heavy boots. His face was red from exposure. Despite the cold he had worked up a sweat, and a frosting of ice coated his forehead. It melted immediately in the warmth of the house, trickling down his temples.

He wiped the moisture away with his sleeve, then added another log to the fire and held his hands out to the blaze, rubbing them briskly to restore circulation.

"I'll make another pot of coffee, if you want some," Hope called as she set the large bowl of stew on the table. "Otherwise, you have a choice of milk or water."

"Water will do." He took the same kitchen chair he had used earlier. Tink, who hadn't been allowed out with Price the second time, left his spot by the fire and came to stand beside Price's chair. With a hopeful look in his eyes, he rested his muzzle on Price's thigh.

Price froze in the midst of ladling a large amount of beef stew into his bowl. He looked down at the soulful brown eyes watching him, and slanted a quick look at Hope. "Am I eating out of his bowl?"

"No, he's just giving you a guilt complex."

"It's working."

"He's had a lot of practice. Tink, come here." She patted her own thigh, but he ignored her, evidently having concluded Price was a softer touch.

Price spooned some of the stew to his mouth, but didn't take the bite. He looked down at Tink. Tink looked at him. Price returned the spoon to his bowl. "For God's sake, do something," he muttered to Hope.

"Tink, come here," she repeated, reaching for the stubborn dog.

Abruptly Tink whirled away from Price, his ears pricked forward as he faced the kitchen door. He didn't bark, but every muscle in his body quivered with alertness.

Price was out of his chair so fast Hope didn't have time to blink. With his left hand he dragged her out of her chair and whirled her behind him, at the same time reaching behind his back, drawing the pistol from his waistband.

She stood paralyzed for a second, a second in which Price seemed to be listening as intently as Tink. Then he put one hand on her shoulder and forced her down on the floor beside the china cabinet, and with a motion of his hand told her to stay there. Noiseless in his stockinged feet, he moved over to the window in the dining area, flattening his back to the wall as he reached it. She watched as he eased his head to the edge of the window, moving just enough so that he could see out with one eye. He immediately drew back, then after a moment eased forward for another look.

A low growl began in Tink's throat. Price made another motion with his hand, and without thinking, Hope reached out and dragged her pet closer to her, wrapping her arms around him, though she didn't know what she could do to keep him from barking. Hold his muzzle, maybe, but he was strong enough that she wouldn't be able to hold him if he wanted to pull free.

What was she doing? she wondered wildly. What if it were law officers out there? They couldn't have tracked Price through the blizzard, but they could be searching any places where he might have found shelter.

But would deputies be on foot, or would they use snowmobiles? She hadn't heard the distinctive roar of the machines, and surely the cold was too dangerous for anyone to be out in it any length of time, anyway.

There were also two other escaped prisoners unaccounted for; would Price be as alarmed if one or both of them were out there? Had he seen anything? There might not be anything out there but a pine cone falling, or a squirrel venturing from its den and knocking some snow off a tree limb.

"I didn't check the cabins," Price muttered savagely to himself. "God damn it, I didn't check the cabins!"

"I locked them up yesterday," Hope said, keeping her voice low.

"Locks don't mean anything." He tilted his head, listening, then made another motion for her to be quiet.

Tink quivered under her hand. Hope trembled too, her thoughts racing. If anyone had stayed last night in one of the cabins, he wasn't a deputy, because a deputy would already have come to the house. That left another escapee. Praying she was right, she clamped her hand around the dog's muzzle and hugged him close to her, whispering an apology.

Tink began fighting her immediately, squirming to get free. "Hold him," Price mouthed silently, easing toward the kitchen door.

From where she crouched beside the china cabinet, Hope couldn't see the door, and she had her hands full with Tink. The door exploded inward, crashing against the wall. She screamed and jumped, and lost her grip on Tink. He tore away from her, his paws sliding on the wood floor as he launched himself toward the unseen intruder.

The shot was deafening. Instinctively she hit the floor, still unable to see what was happening, her ears ringing, the sharp stench of burned cordite stinging her nostrils. A hard thud in the kitchen was followed by the shattering of glass. Her ears cleared enough for her to hear the savage sounds of two men fighting, the grunts and curses and thuds of fists on flesh. Tink's snarls added to the din, and she caught a flash of golden fur as he darted into the fray.

She scrambled to her feet and ran for the rifle. Price knew it was unloaded, but the other person wouldn't.

With the heavy weapon in her hands, she charged back toward the kitchen. As she rounded the cabinets, a heavy body slammed into her, knocking her down. The sharp edge of the counter dug into her shoulder, making her arm go numb, and the rifle slipped from her hand as she landed hard on her back. She cried out in angry pain, grabbing for the rifle and struggling up on one knee.

Price and a stranger strained together in vicious combat, sprawled half on the cabinets. Each man had a pistol, and each had his free hand locked around the other's wrist as they fought for control. They slammed sideways, knocking over her canister set and sending it to the floor. A cloud of flour flew over the room to settle like a powdery shroud over every surface. Price's foot slipped on the flour, and he lost leverage; the stranger rolled, heaving Price to the side. The momentum tore Price's fingers from the stranger's wrist, freeing the pistol.

Hope felt herself moving, scrambling to grab the man's hand, but she felt half paralyzed with horror; everything was in slow motion, and she knew she wouldn't get there before the man could bring the pistol down and pull the trigger.

Tink shot forward, low to the ground, and sank his teeth into the man's leg.

He screamed with pain and shock, and with his other foot kicked Tink in the head. The dog skidded across the floor, yelping.

Price gathered himself and lunged for the man, the impact carrying them both crashing into the table. The table overturned, chairs broke, chunks of meat and potatoes and carrots scattered across the floor. The two men went down, Price on top. The other man's head banged hard against the floor, momentarily stunning him. Price took swift advantage, driving his elbow into the man's solar plexus, and when the man convulsed, gasping, followed up with a short, savage punch under the chin that snapped the man's teeth together. Before he recovered from that, Price had the pistol barrel digging into the soft hollow below his ear.

The man froze.

"Drop the gun, Clinton," Price said in a very soft voice, between gulps of air. *"Now,* or I pull the trigger."

Clinton dropped the gun. Price reached out with his left hand and swiped the weapon back toward himself, pinning it under his left leg. Tucking his own pistol in his waistband, he grabbed Clinton with both hands and literally lifted him off the floor, turning him and slamming him down on his belly. Hope saw Clinton brace his hands, and she stepped forward, shoving the rifle barrel in his face. "Don't," she said.

Clinton slowly relaxed.

Price flicked a glance at the rifle, but he didn't say anything. He wasn't going to reveal it wasn't loaded, Hope realized, but neither would she let on that she knew it. Let him assume she didn't know.

Price dragged Clinton's arms behind his back and held them with one hand, then took the pistol out of his waistband, jamming the barrel against the base of Clinton's skull. "Move one inch," he said in a low, guttural tone, "and I'll blow your fucking head off. Hope." He didn't look at her. "Do you have any thin rope? Scarves will do, if you don't."

"I have some scarves."

"Get them."

She went upstairs and searched through her dresser until she found three scarves. Her knees were trembling, her heart thudding wildly against her ribs. She felt faintly nauseated.

She held on to the railing as she shakily made her way back down the stairs. The two men didn't look as if they had moved, Clinton lying on his belly, Price straddling him. The carnage of wrecked furniture and food surrounded them. Tink was standing at Clinton's head, his muzzle down very close to the man's face, growling.

Price took one of the scarves, twisted it length-wise, and wound it around Clinton's wrists. He jerked the fabric tight and tied it in a hard knot. Then he jabbed the pistol into his waistband once more, took Clinton's pistol from under his knee, and levered himself to his feet. Leaning down, he grabbed the collar of Clinton's coveralls and hauled him to his feet, then slammed him down into the only chair left standing upright. He crouched and secured Clinton's feet to the legs of the chair, using a scarf for each ankle.

Clinton's head lolled back. He was breathing hard, one eye swollen shut, blood leaking from both corners of his mouth. He looked at Hope, standing there pale and stricken, still holding the rifle as if she had forgotten she had it.

"Shoot him," he croaked. "For God's sake . . . shoot him. He's an escaped murderer. I'm a deputy sheriff . . . He took my uniform . . . Damn it, *shoot the bastard!*"

"Nice try, Clinton," Price said, straightening.

"Ma'am, I'm telling the truth," Clinton said. "Listen to me, please."

With one smooth movement Price reached out and tugged the rifle from Hope's nerveless hands. She let it go without a protest, because now that Clinton was tied up, there was no one she could intimidate with the empty weapon.

"Shit," Clinton said, closing his good eye in despair. He sagged against the chair, still breathing hard.

Hope stared at him, fighting off the dizziness that assailed her. He was almost Price's height, but not as muscular. If she was any judge of men's clothing—and after doing all the clothes shopping for first Dylan and now her dad, she had had plenty of experience—Clinton would wear a size fifteen and a half shirt.

Price wasn't unscathed. A lump was forming on his right cheekbone, his left eyebrow was clotted with blood, and his lips were cut in three separate places. He wiped the blood out of his eye and looked at Hope. "Are you all right?"

"Yes," she said, though her shoulder hurt like blue blazes where the cabinet edge had dug in, and she still wasn't at all certain she wasn't going to faint.

"You don't look it. Sit down." He looked around, spotted an unbroken chair, and set it upright. His hand on Hope's shoulder, he pressed her down onto the chair. "Adrenaline," he said briefly. "You always feel weak as hell when the scare's over."

"You broke into one of the cabins, didn't you?" Price asked Clinton. "Built a fire in the fireplace, stayed nice and warm. With the blizzard going on, we wouldn't be able to see the smoke from the chimney. When the weather cleared, though, you had to let the fire go out. Got damn cold, didn't it? But you couldn't head off into the mountains without heavier clothes and some food, so you knew you had to break into the house."

"Good scenario, Tanner," Clinton said. "Is that what you would've done if you hadn't stolen my uniform?" He opened his eye and flicked a look around. "Where's the old man? Did you kill him too?"

Hope felt Price looking at her, assessing her reaction to Clinton's tale, but she merely stared at the captured man without a change in her expression. Maintaining her composure wasn't difficult; she felt numb, absolutely drained. How did Clinton know about her father? Was he from the area? She was not, she thought, cut out to be an action hero.

"Hey." Price squatted in front of her, touching her cheek, folding her hands in his. She blinked, focusing her gaze on him. His brows were drawn together in a small frown, his blue eyes searching as he examined her. "Don't let him play mind games with you, honey. Everything's going to be all right; just relax and trust me."

"Don't listen to him, ma'am," Clinton said.

"You look pretty shaky," Price told her, ignoring Clinton. "Maybe you should lie down for a minute. Come on, let me help you to the couch." He urged her to her feet, his hand under her elbow. As she turned, he uttered a savage curse and hauled her to a halt.

"What?" she said, shaken by the abrupt change in him.

"You said you weren't hurt."

"I'm not."

"Your back is bleeding." His face grim, he force-marched her into her dad's bedroom. He paused to replace the rifle in the rack, then ushered her into the bathroom. After jerking open the curtains so he would have sufficient light, he began unbuttoning her shirt.

"Oh, that. I scraped it on the cabinet edge when I fell." She tried to grab his hands, but he brushed her hands aside and pulled off her shirt, whirling her around so he could examine her back. She shivered, her nipples puckering as the cold air washed over her bare breasts.

He dampened a washcloth and dabbed it on her back, just below her shoulder blade. Hope flinched at the pain.

"You've got a gouge in your back, and from the looks of it, a monster bruise is forming." Gently he continued washing the wound. "You need an ice pack on it, but first I'm going to disinfect that gouge and put a gauze pad over it. Where are your first aid supplies?"

"In the cabinet door over the refrigerator."

"Lie down on the bed. I'll be right back."

He guided her to the bed, and Hope willingly collapsed facedown. She was cold without her shirt, though, and tugged the cover around her.

Price returned in just a moment with the first aid box. Blood was dripping in his eye again, and he paused a minute to wash his own face. Blood immediately trickled down again, and with an impatient curse he tore open an adhesive bandage and plastered it over his eyebrow.

Then, holding the box on his lap, he sat beside Hope and gently dabbed the wound with an antibiotic ointment. As gentle as he was, even the lightest touch was painful. She bore it, refusing to flinch again. He placed a gauze pad over the wound, then covered her with one of her dad's T-shirts.

"Just lie still," he ordered. "I'll get an ice pack."

He improvised an ice pack by filling a Ziploc

plastic bag with ice cubes. Hope jumped when he gently laid it on her back. "That's too cold!"

"Okay, maybe the T-shirt's too thin. Let me get a towel."

He got a towel from the bathroom, and draped it over her in place of the T-shirt. The ice pack was tolerable then, barely.

He pulled the cover up over her, because the room was chilly. "Are you too cold?" he asked, smoothing her hair. "Do you want me to carry you upstairs?"

"No, I'm fine, with the cover over me," she murmured. "I'm sleepy, though."

"Reaction," he said, leaning over and brushing a kiss on her temple. "Take a nap, then. You'll feel fine when you wake up."

"I feel like a wuss right now," she admitted.

"Never been in a fight before?"

"Nope, that was my first one. I didn't like it. I acted like a girl, didn't I?"

He chuckled, his fingers gentle on her hair. "How does a girl act?"

"You know, the way they always do in the movies, screaming and getting in the way."

"Did you scream?"

"Yes. When he kicked in the door. It startled me."

"Fancy that. Did you get in the way?"

"I tried not to."

"You didn't, honey," he said reassuringly. "You kept your head, got the rifle, and held it on him." He kissed her once more, his lips warm on her cool skin. "I'd choose you for my side in any fight. Go to sleep, now, and don't worry about the mess in the kitchen. Tink and I will clean it up. He's already taken care of the beef stew."

She smiled, as he had meant her to, and he eased up from the bed. She closed her eyes, and in a few seconds she heard the quiet click of the door closing.

Hope opened her eyes.

She lay quietly, because the ice pack was easing the soreness in her shoulder. Fifteen minutes on, fifteen minutes off—if she remembered accurately how ice therapy worked. She might need all the flexibility in the shoulder she could muster, and she estimated Price wouldn't check on her for at least an hour. She had a little time to take care of herself.

She heard him moving around in the kitchen.

345

Broken glass tinkled as he swept it up, and she heard the crackle of shattered wood when he picked up the smashed remains of some of her chairs. She didn't hear the captured Clinton utter a sound.

The flour had made quite a mess. Cleaning it up would require vacuuming and mopping, and washing it off everything else would take a lot of time.

Hope threw back the covers and eased off the bed. Silently she opened the closet door and took down one of her dad's sweatshirts, gingerly pulling it on over her head and wincing as her abused shoulder and back muscles protested the movement.

Then she began searching for the bullets.

Half an hour later, she found the box, in the pocket of one of her dad's jackets.

8

Hope had several of her dad's old, no-longer-used neckties dangling from the waistband of her sweatpants when she left the bedroom. The rifle was in her hands.

Clinton was sitting silently, exactly as she had last seen him, not that he had much choice. He opened his good eye when he heard her, the single orb widening as he saw the rifle. He gave a faint, satisfied smile and nodded at her.

Price was standing at the sink, wringing out a dishcloth. He had most of the mess cleaned up, though she was woefully short of furniture now and there were still a few surfaces dusted with flour. He looked up, and whatever he had been about to say died on his lips when she raised the rifle.

"Keep your right hand where I can see it," she said calmly. "Use your left hand to get the pistol out of your waistband. Put it on the cabinet and slide it toward me."

He didn't move. His blue eyes turned hard and glacial. "What in hell do you think you're doing?"

"Taking over," she replied. "Do what I said."

He didn't even glance at the rifle. His mouth set in a grim line, he started toward her.

"I found the bullets," Hope said quickly, before he got close enough to grab the rifle. "In a coat pocket," she added, just so he would know she really had found them.

He stopped. The fury that darkened his face would have terrified her if she hadn't had the rifle.

"The pistol," she prompted.

Slowly, keeping his right hand resting on the sink, he reached behind his back and drew out the pistol. Placing it on the cabinet, he shoved it toward her.

"Don't forget mine," Clinton said from behind her, the words slightly slurred; his damaged mouth and jaw were swelling and turning dark.

"The other one too," Hope said, not flinching from the sulfurous look Price gave her. Silently he obeyed.

"Now step back."

He did. She picked up her pistol and laid down the rifle, because the pistol was more convenient. "Okay, sit down in the chair and put your hands behind you."

"Don't do this, Hope," he said between clenched teeth. "He's a murderer. Don't listen to him. Why would you believe him, for God's sake? Look at him! He's wearing prison coveralls."

"Only because you stole my uniform," Clinton snarled.

"Sit down," Hope told Price again.

"Damn it, why won't you listen to me?" he said furiously.

"Because I heard on the radio about a bus wreck. Two deputies were killed, and five prisoners escaped." Hope didn't take her eyes off his face. She saw his pupils dilate, his jaw harden. "Because your uniform shirt is too small for you. Because you didn't have a wallet, and even though your

349

uniform pants were torn and bloody, you weren't injured anywhere."

"Then what about the service revolver? If I took a deputy's clothes, why wouldn't I have also taken his weapon?"

"I don't know," she admitted. "Maybe you were knocked out during the wreck, and when you regained consciousness, the other prisoners had already escaped and taken the weapons with them. I don't know all the details. All I know is I have a lot of questions, and your answers don't add up. Why did you unload the rifle and hide the bullets?"

He didn't blink. "For safety reasons."

She didn't either. "Bull. Sit down."

He sat. He didn't like it, but her finger was on the trigger and her gaze didn't waver.

"Hands behind your back."

He put them behind his back. Steam was all but coming out of his ears. Staying out of his reach, in case he should whirl suddenly and try to knock the gun out of her hand, she pulled one of the neckties from her waistband and fashioned two loose loops with it. Moving in quickly then, she slipped the loops over his hands and jerked the ends tight. He was already moving, shifting his weight, but he froze in place as the fabric tightened around his wrists.

"Neat trick," he said emotionlessly. "What did you do?"

"Loops, like roping a calf. All I had to do was pull." She wrapped the loose ends between his wrists, tying off each of the loops, and then knotted the tie in place. "Okay, now your feet."

He sat without moving, letting her tie his feet to the chair legs. "Listen to me," he said urgently. "I really am a deputy sheriff. I haven't worked in this county very long and not many people know me."

"Yeah, sure," Clinton snarled. "You killed those two deputies, and you would probably have killed her before you left. Untie me, ma'am, my hands are numb."

"Don't! Listen to me, Hope. You've heard about this guy. He's from around here. That's how he knew you lived with your father. Clinton"—he jerked his head toward the other man—"kidnapped the daughter of a wealthy rancher from this area and asked for a million in ransom. They paid him the money, but he didn't keep his part of the bargain. The girl wasn't where he said he had left her. He was caught when he tried to spend the money, and he's never told where he hid the girl's body. It was all over the news. He was being transferred to a more secure jail, and we thought it was worth a try to put me in with him, maybe get him to talk about it. He can be convicted of murder on circumstantial evidence, but the parents want their child's body found. They've accepted that she's dead, but they want to give her a decent burial. She was seventeen, a pretty little girl he's got buried up in the mountains somewhere, or dumped in an abandoned mine."

"You know a lot of possibilities," Clinton charged, his tone savage. "Keep talking; tell me where you hid her body."

Hope walked into the great room and added more wood to the fire. Then she paused by the telephone, lifting the receiver to check for a dial tone. Nothing.

"What are you doing?" Clinton demanded. "Untie me."

"No," Hope said.

"What?" He sounded as if he couldn't believe what he had heard.

"No. Until the phone service is restored and I can call the sheriff to straighten this out, I figure the best thing to do is keep both of you just the way you are."

There was a stunned moment of silence; then Price threw back his head on a shout of laughter. Clinton stared at her, mouth agape; then his face flushed dark red and he yelled, "You stupid fucking bitch!"

"That's my girl," Price chortled, still laughing. "God, I love you! I'll even forgive you for this, though the guys are going to ride my ass for years about letting a sweet little brown-eyed blonde get the drop on me."

Hope looked at those laughing blue eyes, shiny with tears of mirth, and she couldn't help smiling. "I probably love you too, but that doesn't mean I'm going to untie you."

Clinton recovered himself enough to say, "He's playing you for a fool, ma'am."

" 'Ma'am'?" she repeated. "That isn't what you called me a second ago."

"I'm sorry. I lost my temper." He inhaled raggedly. "It galls me to see you falling for that sweet shit he deals out to every woman."

"I'm sure it does."

"What do I have to do to convince you he's lying?"

"You can't do anything, so you might as well save your breath," she said politely.

Half an hour later Clinton said, "I have to use the bathroom."

"Go in your pants," Hope replied. She hadn't thought about that complication, but she wasn't going to change her mind and untie either one of them. She gave Price an apologetic look, and he winked at her.

"I'm okay for right now. If the phone service isn't restored by nightfall, though, I'll probably be begging you for a fruit jar."

She would bring him one too, she thought. She wouldn't mind performing that service for him at all. She glanced at Clinton. No way; she wouldn't touch his with a pair of tongs.

She checked the phone every half hour, watching as the afternoon sun sank behind the mountains. Clinton squirmed, and she had no doubt he was in misery. Price had to be uncomfortable too, but he didn't let it show. He grinned at her every time he caught her eye, though with his bruised face the grin looked more like a grimace.

Just at twilight, when she lifted the receiver, she heard a dial tone. "Bingo!" she said triumphantly, picking up the phone book to look up the number of the sheriff's department.

Price rattled off the number for her, and though she had been almost certain he was telling the truth, in that moment she knew for certain. Light broke across her face, and she gave him a radiant smile as she punched in the number.

"Sheriff's Department," a brisk male voice said.

"Hello, this is Hope Bradshaw, at the Crescent Lake Resort. I have two men here. One is Price Tanner and the other's name is Clinton. They both claim to be deputies and that the other is a murderer. Can you tell me which is which?"

"Holy shit!" the voice bellowed. "Damn! Shit, I'm sorry, I didn't mean to say that. You say you have both Tanner *and* Clinton?"

"Yes, I do. Which one is your deputy?"

"Tanner is. *How* do you have them? I mean—"

"I'm holding a gun on them," she said. "What does Tanner look like? What color are his eyes?"

The deputy on the line sounded nonplussed.

"His eyes? Ah . . . the subject is approximately six-two, two hundred pounds, dark hair, blue eyes."

"Thank you," Hope said, thankful that law officers were trained to give succinct descriptions. "Would you like to speak with Deputy Tanner?"

"Yes, ma'am, I would!"

Picking up the phone, she carried it as far as she could, but the cord wasn't long enough to reach. "Just a moment," she said, laying down the receiver.

She dashed to the kitchen and got her paring knife. Running back to Price, she knelt and sawed through the fabric binding his wrists, then turned her attention to his ankles while he rubbed feeling back into his hands. "You need a cordless phone," he said. "Or one with a longer cord."

"I'll take care of that the next time I go shopping," she said as she freed his ankles. The kitchen phone was closer, though that cord wasn't long enough to reach either. He hobbled over to it, his muscles stiff from sitting so long in a strained position.

"This is Tanner. Yeah, everything's under control. I'll give a complete briefing when you get here. Are the roads passable yet? Okay." He hung up and hobbled toward her. "The road is still blocked, but they're going to grab a snowplow. They should be here in a couple of hours."

He hobbled past. Hope blinked. "Price?"

"Can't stop to talk," he said, speeding up his hobbling, heading straight toward the bathroom.

Hope couldn't smother her laugh. Clinton glared at her as she walked past him to hang up the phone in the great room. She still had the paring knife in her hand. She paused and looked at him consideringly, and something must have shown in her face, because he blanched.

"Don't," he said as she started toward him, and then he began to yell.

"YOU CUT HIM," Price said, his tone disbelieving. "You really cut him."

"He had to know I meant business," Hope said. "It was just a teeny cut, nothing to make such a fuss about. Actually, it was an accident; I didn't intend to get that close, but he jumped."

That wasn't all Clinton had done; he had also lost control of his bladder. And then he had begun talking, babbling as fast as he could, yelling for Price, saying anything to keep her from cutting him again. Price had called the sheriff's department and relayed the information, which they hoped was accurate.

IT WAS AFTER MIDNIGHT. They lay in bed, their arms around each other. She held an ice pack to his cheek; he held another one on her back.

"I meant it, you know," Price said, kissing her forehead, "about loving you. I know everything happened too fast, but . . . I know what I feel. From the minute I opened my eyes and saw your face, I wanted you." He paused. "So . . . ?"

"So?" she repeated.

"So, you 'probably' love me too, huh?"

"Probably." She nestled more comfortably against him. "Definitely."

"Say it!" he ordered under his breath, his arms tightening around her.

"I love you. But we really should take our time, get to know each other—"

He gave a low laugh. "Take our time? It's a little late for that, isn't it?"

She had no answer, because too much had happened in too short a time. She felt as if the past day had been weeks long. Thrown together as they had been under extreme circumstances, she had seen him in a multitude of situations, and she knew her first dazed, deliriously joyous impression of him had been accurate. She felt as if she had known him immediately, primitive instinct recognizing him as her mate.

"Marry me, Hope. As soon as possible. The chances we've taken, we've probably hit the baby jackpot." His voice was lazy, seductive.

She lifted her head from his shoulder, staring at him through the darkness. She saw the gleam of his teeth as he smiled, and once again she felt that jolt of awareness, of recognition. "All right," she whispered. "You don't mind?"

"Mind?" He took her hand and carried it to his crotch. He was hard as a rock. "I'm raring to go, honey," he whispered, and his voice was trembling a little, as it had earlier when they discussed the possibility. "All you have to do is say the word, and I'll devote myself to the project."

"Word," she said, joyfully giving herself up to the inevitable.

Visit the
Simon & Schuster Web site:
www.SimonSays.com

and sign up for our
mystery e-mail updates!

Keep up on the latest
new releases, author appearances,
news, chats, special offers, and more!
We'll deliver the information
right to your inbox — if it's new,
you'll know about it.

Printed in the United States
By Bookmasters